To my dear friend Lois —
With aloha —
Linda Lauterman
May 2005

Stain

A What if? Novel

by

Linda Lanterman

authorHOUSE™

1663 LIBERTY DRIVE, SUITE 200
BLOOMINGTON, INDIANA 47403
(800) 839-8640
WWW.AUTHORHOUSE.COM

This novel is a work of fiction. People, events and situations in this story are products of the author's imagination. Gloria Macapagal Arroyo, the President of the Philippine Islands, and Kate Gordon, the Mayor of Olongapo, are real, but mentioned in fictitious circumstances merely to frame the narrative.

First published by AuthorHouse 01/28/05

ISBN: 1-4208-1813-9 (e)
ISBN: 1-4208-1812-0 (sc)

Printed in the United States of America
Bloomington, Indiana

This book is printed on acid-free paper.

I thank the following people for their assistance and encouragement.

Doug, John, Chhanseda, Jeff, Angela and Bentley, Davis, Alexa and Luke, who are my greatest joys.

Jan Edwards, Janice Matsumura, Judy Mutch, Marilyn Shodiss, and Jane Stefani, the remaining members of the Los Altos Tennis and Philosophy Group.

Dr. John Lanterman, Jeff Lanterman, Esq., Margaret Abe, Paul Gouveia, Jim and Metta Keenan, Dennis Mock-Chew, Wallis Leslie, Larry Hutchinson, deckhand on Shogun 2, Minda, Rudy and Christine Calamayan, Lilia Alcon, Nestor Alcon, and Jan Provan for their friendship and their wealth of information.

Livvy Coupe, Kathy Ryan, Ann Elliott, Joel Nelson, Captain Amy Fine, Mary Rosseau, Baron R. Birtcher and Victoria Kalman for their encouragement and editing assistance.

Thanks also to my brothers, Dennis, Jeff and Dean Coupe for their legal and military expertise. And my thanks to Walt Coupe, Art Ryan and all high school US History and Government teachers who work to inculcate the ideals of democracy in future generations. And to Margaret, taken too soon, who lives in my heart.

Also by Linda Lanterman

The Writing Lesson
Not Nice
Release Me
Transition in Green

Prologue

March 2004

Cynthia Fields, Maintenance Manager, rode her bicycle the short block to the tennis club and found a Pacific Gas and Electric van in the parking lot. Odd. She just got off the phone with P.G. and E. The call came from here? They needed a key. Something about an electrical problem with the pool pump had triggered a warning at their plant.

A long strand of chestnut hair, colored by Clairol, whipped across her eyes. The solitary gust chilled her. She stood for a moment, one hand on the handlebars, the other smoothed her hair. Something was wrong.

"Hello? Hello!"

No one answered. The van looked empty. Red blotches popped out on her cheeks. Anger replaced fear. She unlocked the gate and shoved the heavy door open wide enough to push her bike inside. Two men and a woman stood there, too close. They invaded her personal space.

"What's going…?"

"Cynthia Fields?"

They grabbed her bike and flashed badges and gave orders and hustled her into the deserted clubhouse. Confusion seized Cynthia, then panic. By the time she screamed they were inside. They forced her into a chair. Their words pelted her like hailstones. She heard her own voice, her Texas accent, without knowing what words she used.

She remembered one of the men stayed outside. In case someone came to play tennis? To swim laps? Keys? These people had keys. Why had they called her? Questions. They had lots of questions. Nothing made sense. They mentioned her grown children, her son in New Mexico and her daughter in Colorado.

Cynthia felt her heart contract, squeezed to the size of a walnut. She couldn't breathe. She grew faint. A cup of water appeared in her hand. She sipped but couldn't swallow. She concentrated. The questions didn't make sense. The water spilled in her lap. The woman took over from the man. She talked instead of asking questions. Her voice sounded calm, heavy. It weighed on Cynthia and made her feel helpless. Trapped.

"Why me?" Did she say those words aloud? They didn't answer. It didn't matter. She knew why. It was so unfair. Such a small, senseless thing. What any decent person would do.

Her ordeal lasted twenty-seven minutes, but she had no sense of time. Cynthia walked her bike home. She still trembled when she went into her house. Her husband Jason saw her disconnected, anguished look. He held her and talked to her and told her it wasn't her fault. It took weeks for her nightmares to diminish. There was no one they could call.

They had told her to act normal, as if nothing happened. After a while she found she could. She swept the incident into an unexamined corner of her mind and left it there to rot.

War is not a value or a tool. War is the failure of reason.

> — Aurora Druid, Leader in the Democracy
> Reformation of 2010-2024,
> Quoting her grandmother

Chapter 1

Washington D.C., January 2004

Secretary of Homeland Security Thomas Peaks stood with his hand on the knob of the closed door to his outer office. "Time is of the essence. Roll it up in two or three days, no more. If we miss some, go to the next names on the list. Stop the nonsense. We go for shock value. Shut down the noise. Can't have irresponsible nobodies slowing our efforts and confusing real Americans."

Undersecretary Sylvia Mitchell had one last question. "Without time for individual work-ups, how do we make the selections?"

"Go with the party loyalists' recommendations. Keep it quiet. Have our people ask the locals who's their big pain. We want low level, community level folks. Don't give reasons."

Sylvia frowned. "We'll roll up Republicans as well as others if that's all we say."

"Sylvia." Secretary Peaks tilted his head as if he were talking to an idiot. "Tell them we want troublemakers, anti-administration people, enemies of freedom. Don't say why. We pick up a Republican or two, it won't hurt. Looks evenhanded."

He showed his undersecretary out and returned to his desk. He gathered the papers he'd shown her. The documents had yellow cover sheets, each with a chain of custody routing slip. Each page of text had TOP SECRET stamped top and bottom.

TOP SECRET (EYES ONLY)

NATIONAL SECURITY POLICY DIRECTIVE
FROM: Department of Homeland Security
OFFICE OF THE SECRETARY, THE HONORABLE THOMAS PEAKS
SUBJECT: DETENTION OF US CITIZENS
DATE: January 10, 2004
REFERENCES: (SEE ANNEX A, RE: CIPA, Classified Information Procedures Act and ICRCA, International Committee and of Red Cross Access)

BACKGROUND: The United States of America has declared War on Terror. Recent demonstrations, public agitation and radical exhortations play into the hands of terrorists and undermine the War on Terror:

US citizens, while enjoying the right of freedom of speech, never have had the right to endanger fellow citizens or their homeland.

The first demand of a free people upon their government is the right to be secure and safe from enemies, including terrorists and those who support terrorists.

The Government of the United States has the duty to protect its citizens and their property, and guarantee, to the extent possible, the safety of its citizens in their homes and in all public places.

NSC, DOC, DOS meet with President to determine if the following actions are necessary by Executive Order:

1. Individuals who are in policy making and leadership roles in the organizing, coordination and/or execution of public demonstrations which are determined by the Department of Homeland Security to be disruptive of US anti-terror efforts be detained for investigation of criminal activities or as material witnesses.

2. Key communicators known to oppose the US War on Terror be interviewed and/or detained for investigation until such time as the War on Terror is deemed won, or until released by Director of Homeland Security.

3. American citizens and others arrested or detained under these findings shall be held outside the geographic US at suitable facilities such as Guantanamo Bay, Cuba, Singapore, or Olongapo City/Subic Bay, Philippine Islands.

Briefings to follow: Constitutional challenges are anticipated and will be addressed in coordination with DOS and OGC/DOJ.

COORDINATION: Coordination: DOS: concur/ nonconcur_____;

DOD: concur/nonconcur_____; NSA: concur/ nonconcur_____;

WHGC: concur/nonconcur_____; DHS: concur/ nonconcur___.

SIGNED this Tenth Day of January 2004, at 0900 hours.

BY THE PRESIDENT OF THE UNITED STATES

Approved_____ Disapproved_____

TOP SECRET/ EYES ONLY

SUMMARY of Briefings on Internal Directive of 10 January 2004, Presidential FINDINGS AND CONCLUSIONS:

(Over the period of February and March 2004)

Although relations with the Philippines deteriorated over the past few years, the consensus deems Subic Bay most suitable for the detention of US citizens. Secret negotiations with the Philippine Government have led to an agreement for the US to rent space for detention facilities and the construction of appropriate facilities. The Philippine Government will grant basic jurisdiction over the location with the US exercising proprietary law enforcement powers over detainees. The former US Navy base at Subic Bay has a long-standing presence. The Philippine government will continue to operate the former base, with the US constructing and commanding only the operation of the detention facilities on the outskirts of Olongapo City. President Arroyo needs foreign investment in her country, particularly now in a presidential election year. Mountainous jungle terrain surrounds the bay, geographically isolating it. In the past, tribesmen in the surrounding jungle had a history of hostility to all outsiders. Although the area has developed and the population grown, residual anti-government feelings may exist. Residents would have little motive to assist US detainees. New facilities constructed for men's and women's detention centers eventually would revert to the government of the Philippines as a partial inducement for cooperation. These facilities could supply the additional school facilities, mentioned in Olongapo's strategic plan, in the city's application to the World Bank. The US presence could aid in the expansion of the water supply system and assist in rehabilitation of the power distribution system as well.

RECOMMENDATIONS:

Appropriations from DHS/ DOD/ DOS, NTE (not to exceed) one hundred million dollars in cash, military equipment and field advisors be supplied to the Philippine government at once.

Plausible denial applies to the extent possible, the purpose of the Olongapo facilities should be kept confidential and a plausible cover story developed and selectively leaked. OR, conversely, tell the complete truth about the facilities. Americans detained by Americans should be of little concern to the government and people of the Philippines.

Concept plan to be developed with CIA, DOS, DOJ, OGC coordination.

The men's and women's facilities should have separate and distinct administrators, staffs, guards and other workers.

While the outside world may know about the facilities, the Department of Homeland Security intends to keep the location secret from the detainees as a further inducement for cooperation. Only DOS nonconcurs.

Construct men's and women's facilities far enough apart so that no sight or sound from one can be detected at the other. (The Subic Bay area's mountainous jungle terrain is highly suitable.)

Station a military medic at each center.

Require running water and soap at each camp.

Require at least half the MPs at the women's camp be women, with some women assigned to every shift.

All personal items shall be confiscated, except ID tags and eye glasses. Include jewelry, wedding rings, pens, pencils, etc.

Each detainee receives standard issue clothing, mess gear, etc.

All briefing groups agreed Guantanamo too well known, too sensitive and too close to US. Constructing new facilities like those at Guantanamo impractical due to existing unfavorable publicity and Cuban hostility.

All groups reached consensus and recommend immediate implication.

DATE: 15 March 2004

COORDINATION: Concur/Nonconcur

TOP SECRET/EYES ONLY

* * *

The President had initialed the first document and circled Concur on the second. That was all that was necessary. His fingerprints were all over both papers.

Chapter 2

Subic Bay, Philippine Islands

July 2004

A battered, twenty-six foot fishing boat nosed away from a pier in Subic Bay and headed for the open sea. The engine ran smoothly although smoky diesel fumes accompanied its rattle. Three rods extended from rod holders. No lines trailed. Hutch Okekope, his wife, Clarita, and their two young daughters sat in silence and watched the sky, sea birds, the lights coming on in Olongapo, anything but their cargo.

Two bodies rolled in frayed plastic tarps and tied with yellow nylon line lay on the deck. The boat headed straight out to sea while the sun descended through the squalls on the horizon. When the dusk of the sunset's afterglow gave them enough cover, Hutch put the engine in neutral. Clarita pulled leis from a plastic grocery bag and handed one to each of her daughters. The youngest, played with an origami crane. When she unfolded it and couldn't get it refolded, Clarita leaned down and helped her. "If you want to keep it, put it in your pocket, Momi."

Hutch led prayers to the Christian god. He offered a late blossoming sprig from a coffee tree and a handful of his roasted beans, then began a solemn Hawaiian chant. He didn't remember all the parts, but he did his best. His deep tones and rhythms floated upon the swells. The sea listened. A light breeze caressed the boat and dried Clarita's tears. Hutch stopped, opened the transom door and pulled on the nylon line that secured the bodies then rested his hand on the closest one. He took a slow, deep breath. "Aloha. Until later." He struggled, but no other words came. He nudged the smaller one into the water first then, with two pats, the second one. "Later, brah." He pinched his nose hard before he turned to face his family.

"They are together in the sunset and the sea. What they wanted."

A triangle fin sliced the inky surface and circled the boat.

"Daddy, look!"

"Mano. Tiger shark. A good sign, girls. It's a good sign. The ancients approve. Mano came to tell us this is right."

Chapter 3

Forest Vista Tennis Club
Los Altos, California

March 2006

They were the only ones there. Six women spoke in turn, short informal anecdotes, funny and serious. They told their memories of Madison and how she'd touched their lives. Sue Riddle mentioned Madison's big serve, hard-hitting game and how Madison liked to play with her as a partner in the inter-club tournaments.

"I'm the lob queen. I know it," said Sue. "I play a softer, finesse game. I go for placement. The reason Maddy liked me for a partner was to keep our opponents off-balance. They had trouble getting their rhythm against us."

Forest Vista, a neighborhood, proprietary membership club, had three tennis courts, a nice pool and barbecue area, kiddy pool and playground. The small clubhouse was dim and cool. Dusty Jack Kramer rackets decorated the walls. Coffee, tea, fresh fruit and homemade apricot scones on fine china rested in front of each person at two round tables pulled together. The women helped themselves to steaming servings of a mushroom and asparagus frittata. Seven mysterious, purple foil bags tied with green ribbons decorated a side table where a small basket sat on a printed sheet of paper that read Donations for Leilani and Momi, (Hutch and Clarita's girls) and for Lupe. The women brought spring flowers, fine linens and heavy sterling from home for their simple memorial.

Tall, slender Cynthia Fields, the last to speak, dabbed her eyes, smiled and stood with her back to the sunny windows that looked out on the lawn and trees. She wore a flowing, light chiffon dress with tracings of orange poppies and green stems. Around her neck she had a polished agate set in silver suspended from a silver chain. On her right hand she wore a large milky amber stone, in a silver setting of vines and leaves. On her left, she had her simple gold wedding band. She opened her notebook, but closed it and spoke her mind.

"These memories are treasures, gifts of joy. I recall the day the oleanders spoke Chinese."

Kate said, "I remember that day! Court 3, by the road. The oleanders hadn't been cut back yet."

"Yes!" Sue beamed and brought her hands together in a silent clap. "Maddy was there."

Cynthia noticed the puzzled looks from those who hadn't been present. "We were on the court, between points." She waved her arms as she spoke. "A light breeze moved clusters of white blossoms atop tall, graceful branches, in perfect unison to the voices of two elderly Chinese ladies who strolled by. We couldn't see the Chinese women until they walked down the street. In the meantime, we stopped and listened to the flowers converse."

She saw benign smiles from those who didn't share the memory. "You had to be there."

"I think it was Cantonese," said Kate.

Cynthia straightened her sleeve. "Of all the wonderful memories, I want to add to what Sue said about the Murder Mystery party she and Kent hosted years ago. At the end of the evening, Kent announced, 'Did we invite the right people, or what!' Remember that? We had such fun because each of us played his or her role to the hilt. And, of all the players, —"

"Ev was the murderer!" Kate said. "We didn't know until the end."

Cynthia's chin rose a fraction. "Of all the players," she said with a look that dared another interruption. "Of all the players, Maddy became her character. She stepped into her role as the flighty lingerie salesperson two days before the party. She called to me on the tennis court and asked me to come by her shop. It is in that spirit of fun, not sadness, I suggest we take a couple minutes of silence so we each can reflect on the lives of Ev and Madison Druid." But Cynthia didn't bow her head. She moved quickly and slid a manila folder before each woman.

"What?" Kate looked up. Cynthia stabbed the words printed on the folder with her index finger with a glare and a smile at the same time.

Keep silent.
Keep quiet until I start.
Do not mention this packet. Play your roles as
yourselves.
Trust me, please. They listen.

Kate read the words, dropped her scone in her lap, reached for her cup, then pulled back her hand without it. Sue swallowed twice, nearly choked. Leslie English coughed. Sydney Miramoto, head bent, looked around the room. Peach White stared into some middle distance only she saw. It was all too familiar. Strange things few Americans imagined could happen here had become commonplace. The terror alerts every month, postponing the election, identification cards with fingerprints, no-fly lists, do not employ lists, no appeals, friends spying on friends, loyalty oaths, all took hold without much public knowledge and no public input. While the Federal Government gave official lip service to the Bill of Rights, the courts found little time to ensure the rights Americans had previously enjoyed. When a federal judge challenged a new regulation, the Congress moved quickly and took away the jurisdiction of the federal courts. Yes, it had become too familiar. Sue rose silently and brought the ornate silver coffee server to the tables. She refilled cups. Peach brought the scones, again in silence. Cynthia waited two and a half minutes, cleared her throat and began.

"We want to understand Madison's death, an untimely, political death. We could have hidden in the weeds two years ago. I hid for a while, I admit. But in the end, we didn't. We found our courage in her detention and death. We discovered who we are." Cynthia hugged her notebook to her chest and looked at each woman in turn. "I'm so proud of you. You've been strong." She pressed her lips together and drew a deep breath. Her Texas drawl intensified. Her voice wavered, but she continued.

"I have much more than the summary you wanted. It took all this time, even with Leslie's help. I couldn't have done the job without her. She organized the notes Maddy's family copied for me and helped decipher things." Cynthia described how Maddy wrote on scraps of paper, sometimes used paper she'd written on earlier, once the thin cardboard of the inside of a box of tampons. Another time she used pages from a washing machine manual.

"Leslie was the one who found Tom Meese, one of the contractors with the Across the Board company in Olongapo. He sent a long letter. I also had help from a couple media people who wish to remain anonymous." Cynthia waited a moment and watched her friends' faces. Sydney put a finger to her lips. Kate covered her mouth with the fingers of her left hand. Cynthia saw them. She plunged ahead and skipped over the questions in the eyes of a couple others.

"I had the *tough* job of meeting Hutch and Clarita and the girls in Hawaii when they made a visit to Kona." She paused again and grinned broadly. "We 'talked story' for hours and hours. We visited Hutch's family's coffee farm. We drove by the little house that

Ev and Madison had owned, and we took a boat ride down to Red Hill.

"Peach had the most success with the five former detainees. They really didn't talk much to me. They trusted her more. She'd been there with them.

"Most of Madison's notes chronicled events without any elaboration. More like short outlines. She'd write the date, what happened to whom without the rich commentary we associated with her. I wanted it in story form so we'd remember it better.

"When Maddy wrote comments, I included them. I made suppositions, of course. Madison wrote of a dream, a warning, she had. It's in here. I believe the vivid dreams I had about wind and waves and rain, coconut palms and voices laughing, crying. They were germane, I believe, so I included them. When I introduce someone you don't know, understand that it's someone I know or met or heard about someway or another." She sniffed, dabbed her nose with a tissue. "If I'm going to get through this, I need to keep going and not stop. Jot down any questions for later.

"Remember, I'm the one you laugh at when I say things like the cantaloupe tells us where to cut without dragging a seed through its flesh." She laughed a nervous, edgy sound. The others exchanged looks. Of course they would interrupt, ask questions, laugh and cry with her. They always had.

Leslie sat on the hearth and dumped the contents of a shredder into the fireplace as unobtrusively as she could and returned to her seat. Cynthia continued. "I'm the one you ask to demonstrate how to dice a mango with the skin in place, then serve without the skin. I believe nature talks to us when we listen and observe. I believe in intuition, connections and signs. So, yes, I've taken liberties. Some things at the edge of my consciousness did not register immediately. It took me a while to make connections, to weave this story."

She paused and in a louder voice, the serious one that reverted to her southern drawl, she said, "So what we have is fiction, technically. This the only copy." Cynthia glared at the others and held up the manuscript in both hands. "This is the end of it. I'll read it aloud for our last good-bye to our friends, then we'll burn it." She waved her hand toward the fireplace. "You're my witnesses."

The women sorted out their inner thoughts, and Cynthia's voice returned to normal. "I want to thank Lupe Verdad, Hutch and Clarita Okakope and Peach, especially. Hutch, Clarita and Lupe, who risked their lives, certainly their liberty, each time they carried out one of Madison's scribbled notes. And, Peach, for giving up her comfortable life, for placing herself in jeopardy, for her diary of the time she spent with the Red Cross in the Philippines and for showing us the deepest meaning of friendship."

Cynthia paused and Peach, downcast, spoke to the tabletop, "I wish we'd talked more. We worried about exposing our friendship. Maybe I took my Red Cross obligation too seriously."

Cynthia walked behind Peach's chair and put a hand on the other woman's shoulder. "I know you don't talk much about your experience, Peach, but your diary should go to the Library of Congress or to the Smithsonian, along with Madison's notes, for history."

"Fat chance." Sydney Miramoto's voice was audible only to Kate Yoshihara and Leslie English who sat beside her.

Awash in silent tears, Peach removed her steamy glasses from her lovely, round face and stared out the window, toward the light. Sue handed her a pink linen napkin. Peach patted Sue's hand and pulled the napkin over her face.

Cynthia moved back to the front of the room. "Newspapers, bits of conversations with retired military people, fragments of all sorts. I don't know that I would have done anything differently, but nature or some force, some higher power understood what was happening. I gathered together events like a puzzle. Shadow memories, things seen without thought, returned in dreams. My fingers worked with my mind. I'd test, fit or reject, until a cutout fell into place. I had to do it. I owed Madison. Owed Ev and Maddy both." She swallowed hard, opened her notebook and began.

* * *

"The trouble began and ended with coffee grounds. Two years ago. Nature's little joke. Many believe this, but the trouble didn't end. The story never ends."

Chapter 4

Maddy and Ev's Story

Los Altos, March 18, 2004

Neither Cynthia nor husband Jason drank coffee, but Cynthia recycled with religious fervor. She grew heritage tomatoes and composted and collected used coffee grounds from the Sunnyvale Starbucks. Cynthia and the members of the Forest Vista Tennis and Philosophy Club lived in Los Altos, close to where the towns mingled. The women saved Thursday mornings for tennis and talk.

Madison, present in spirit, christened the group years earlier. But that was before she and Ev moved to the Sierra Foothills, before their detention, before friends realized they would never see them again.

* * *

An early spring shower forced the Tennis and Philosophy group to adjourn from the Forest Vista courts to Starbucks at Homestead and Hollenbeck.

"I'll drive," said Cynthia. "I can fit four."

"Oh, Sue, would you mind driving, too? We need to talk about the Republican precinct lists." Kate opened the passenger side of Sue's car without waiting for her answer. "This will save us a phone call."

Sue shrugged and pulled out her keys. Cynthia shot a look at Peach but said nothing.

"What's so important about precinct lists?" Peach said. "They're public documents."

Kate laughed, ignored the question and said, "We'll take Maddy."

Maddy wasn't there, of course. Gone three years, Madison and Evert Druid moved away and split their time between Auburn in the Sierra foothills and Kona, Hawaii. Madison, a retired professor and a master in the use of the teachable moment often attended in a spirit so palpable the others spoke for her, of her, and sometimes to her.

The women descended upon the undersized Starbucks with military precision. Cynthia and Kate placed the orders while Peach and Sue commandeered a table and rearranged chairs. No one in the place took particular notice.

Women in tennis togs move throughout the Peninsula towns. The *San Francisco Chronicle's* Herb Caen, dead many years, once wrote, "You always know the Los Altos woman at the funeral. She's the one in tennis clothes."

Behind the counter the clerk took Cynthia's order. She ordered an organic spiced tea for herself, a double latte for Sue and coffee for Peach and Kate.

"Peach, did you want the 100 % Kona or something cheaper?"

"Kona coffee, please."

Cynthia knew the young woman in the Starbucks apron and asked, "May I pick up your coffee grounds today?"

"You sure can. I'll bring them out when you're ready."

Cynthia caught Sue's smirk and glanced at Peach who said, "Why on earth would you… "

Cynthia rushed her words. "Makes great compost."

"Starbucks has a new policy to recycle their used coffee grounds," Kate said.

Cynthia turned back to the counter. Kate, in a hushed aside, said, "I recycle, but I don't go that far. By the way, isn't Hawaii a Democratic state?"

"Grounds for gardeners," said Cynthia, whose hearing was excellent. "Their Green Team came up with the idea."

"Okay," said Kate, her voice neutral. She glanced away. Kate stood almost a head taller than the others. Peach and Cynthia found her difficult to read sometimes. Sue bit her lip to suppress a grin. But Kate continued.

"How do you rationalize your psychological counseling with your religion, Sue? I mean one is dogma and the other requires at least some reason and logic. One is— "

Sue raised her hand and cut off the onslaught of words. "Boxes! I don't rationalize it for a moment. I don't. I keep mind boxes. When I open one I close the others. The open one gets my full attention. As long as I stay busy and happy, I don't have to reconcile things." Quiet Sue surprised them with her retort.

"Oh," said Kate. "Guess that was a little out of line. Sorry."

The women settled at the table, hands around warm mugs. Everyone talked at once. Spun by quick minds, ideas circled over the table, debated, tested and probed. Divergent backgrounds forged the respect and loyal friendship that tennis began. They sprang from different politics. Their religious leanings varied from Christian Right to Judaism to Buddhism to something the others called New Age. Kate graduated from Cal, Sue from San Jose State U., Peach from the University of Oregon and Cynthia from the University of Texas. Peach, Sue and Kate held advanced degrees. Cynthia devoted herself to her children and volunteered in the community. Peach, a semi-retired teacher, kept one adult education history class each quarter. Although Sue occasionally disagreed with certain policies and practices, she and her husband taught Sunday school at their Baptist church. She worked for Santa Clara County as a marriage and family therapist. Kate, a concert pianist, taught music to advanced piano students, by audition only. They all were in long-term marriages or commitments, except Peach who thought of herself as a widow. Sue, the counselor, had suggested that kind of thinking wasn't healthy. Peach's husband of thirty-nine years retired, divorced her and married a woman he met over the Internet. Peach didn't listen, so Sue let it go.

So soon after California's primary, politics and California's general election became their focus this particular Thursday. "I'd love to hear Madison dissect the election," said Sue. She often nodded or rolled her eyes, smiled or frowned, and sometimes made non-committal sounds that the others interrupted as they wished.

"I hope the proposition for an open primary will qualify for the November ballot," said Sue. "I remember Madison's talking about it. Said we'd tend to get more moderate candidates if we had an open primary."

"Sue! You're a Republican. The party is opposed. Even the Democrat Party doesn't want it," said Kate.

"I agree with Sue," said Peach. "Otherwise people tend to get intellectually lazy, intellectually dishonest. They yell. Democracy depends on a free, open and robust exchange of ideas, not insults."

Kate looked at the ceiling. "You sound like Maddy."

"We co-authored a high school government text, remember? State Board adopted it. It's on the approved list." Peach's chin jutted with pride. "At least until their next round of approvals."

Sue sat back and smiled broadly, as if saying *You never fail to remind us*. Peach caught Sue's look. She took the hint and sipped her coffee.

"It'll probably be purged this time around." Cynthia spoke into her hand. Kate frowned at her.

"Kate, I favor an open primary, and I'm a Democrat." Cynthia laughed. "Thought you knew that."

"Last I heard you sounded more like a Green Party person," Kate said.

Sue derailed the political talk. "The family coming for Easter, Cynthia?"

And so it went until Cynthia remarked on the time and said, "The four of us should go out more. It's been fun."

When everyone rose to leave, Peach made a pronouncement that changed the morning's tenor.

"Oh, I ran into Leslie yesterday. Would you believe she thinks you're a better player than I am? Cynthia, I mean, I play so much more than you. My game is great, really at its peak. Don't know where she got such an idea."

Cynthia said nothing. Peach didn't notice. Peach often missed the blood she drew. Sue and Kate watched Cynthia's eyes widen. Her right eyebrow hopped once and amusement played across her face. Peach had the habit of floating outlandish statements, or rude ones, and glancing into space.

Sue said, "Kate, can you ride with the others? Just realized I need to run some errands on the way home." Sue dashed to her car with a wave and took off. The others piled into Cynthia's car and returned to the parking lot at Forest Vista.

"Yikes!" Peach looked at her watch. "Didn't realize it was so late. My last Red Cross training session's today." She said her good-byes and left.

"Red Cross?" Cynthia looked at Kate.

"She was in the Red Cross years ago. Rejoined to give her more to do than tennis and worry."

Kate and Cynthia talked for several more minutes in the tennis club's parking lot. They still chatted as Sue drove into the parking lot.

"Guess you didn't really have errands to run," said Kate when Sue stepped from her car.

"I did, but I needed to come back here, too. I left my swim stuff in my locker the other day."

Kate did not let go. "You could have given Peach a ride back."

Sue said, "Peach makes my teeth itch, if you must know."

"Your professional opinion, Sue?" Kate laughed.

"Well, Peach sure splattered a batch of pigs feet and hog jowls on my morning." Cynthia feigned disappointment.

"Cynthia, you have as good a game as Peach any day." Kate frowned. "I'm surprised Peach would say that."

"Amen," said Sue.

"She plays a lot of tennis," said Cynthia. "Maybe we frustrate her sometimes. We talk while we play. I think she gets impatient when we discuss things that don't interest her. And, she has a lot on her plate, battling diabetes, the divorce, then Jack's remarriage."

"She talks too, but it's always the same. "She complains so much," said Kate, unwilling to let the subject pass. "Speaking of that, what about her line calls recently? She needs new glasses."

Sue's eyes met Cynthia's in mutual understanding. They knew Kate shared Peach's bluntness.

Sue plunged ahead to a new subject. "Wonder how Maddy is doing in Hawaii? Must not have been home long. Weren't they in Kona all winter?"

"Not sure she's there yet. Can't keep up with their schedule. We should plan a trip over," said Cynthia allowing her Texas accent free rein. "They've invited us."

"We could all show up at once," said Kate. "What a blast we'd have."

Sue rolled her eyes. "Better call first."

* * *

The women at Forest Vista who sat with their elegant china cups and linen napkins exchanged looks. No one appeared offended. Lips turned up in remembrance and understanding of a time from another universe. It seemed a time of trivial innocence and silliness as they thought about it. Cynthia paused for a sip of cold tea. She saw a sunbeam bounce from the pool outside and land in an empty chair. Cynthia tilted her head to it and continued her story.

* * *

At home, Cynthia noticed that her Starbucks coffee grounds weighed more than usual as she carried the plastic sack from her trunk through the door to the backyard. She'd dig the grounds into her compost pile later.

Two days passed before Cynthia hefted the garbage bag with one hand and spun it to untwist the top. She unleashed pungent, fermented vapors. A rose-scented air current caught the smell and whispered to an ancient goddess. The goddess awoke and gave birth to conspiracy. The bag contained more than coffee grounds.

Cynthia wrinkled her nose. Frown lines of concentration deepened on her forehead. Garbage! Ordinary garbage lay mixed in the dark grounds. She looked closer. "I need to call the police." She brushed away coffee grounds and carried the things into the house to show Jason.

The goddess laughed. Morning Glories bounced with her merriment. Cynthia would have noticed or at least appreciated the bobbing flowers, but she concentrated fully on what she must do next.

"Jason! Look what I found in the coffee grounds."

Chapter 5

Hawaii, March 18, 2004

Thursday afternoon north winds swirled through the mountains on the Big Island. A saffron finch fell dead from the sky. A small boy found it under the coffee trees. He brushed the bright, soft feathers with his fingers and confronted death for the first time. The child carried the bird to his favorite place, a boulder of black, pockmarked lava. He stacked small, yellow-tinged lava rocks around and over the finch. He stood a broken stem of coffee blossoms in the rocks, and the Earth sighed.

In the season of Kona snow when the hillsides turn white with coffee blossoms, volcanologists issued their weekly report. The summit of Mauna Loa continued its expansion. Lava oozed from Kilauea into the ocean as it had for years. The seismographs recorded several tremors, nothing unusual. The monthly tests of emergency sirens, tsunami warnings, screamed at noon, on schedule.

Even a few earthquake-proof Californians transplanted to Kona remarked on three early morning quakes in three months that had awakened them. They asked themselves, Who would live on an active volcano? Perhaps someone who knows Pele or her friends. The Trade winds heard the questioners' dreamy answer to their own question. *We would. Criticize us when we're dead. For now it sounds too much like jealousy.*

Chapter 6

Los Altos the same day

Cynthia called the police. She persevered on the phone for half an hour, mostly on hold. The Los Altos police suggested she contact Sunnyvale Public Safety. She did. Public Safety would send someone to pick up the cards in a day or two, when they had an officer free. Sunnyvale had no police report of these particular items. Perhaps she should call Starbucks.

"Lady, we have a stack of credit cards here," said a coffee shop employee. "People are always forgetting them." Cynthia envisioned a harried clean-up man from his tone of voice, but she tried.

"There are family pictures, too. And a social security card, insurance card. Stuff like that. For two people."

"Money?"

"No money."

"Figures."

Cynthia didn't suggest a Starbucks thief. She didn't know what happened. A thief could have been a customer as easily as an employee. It might not be a case of theft at all. She thumbed through the directory with the phone nestled between her ear and her shoulder. She found a Sunnyvale listing for Ty and Suzanne Forrester. She checked the credit card again. The spelling was the same. She called.

"Yes, lost my wallet two months ago. Toss the credit card. I cancelled that. Have a new account. Cut it up, then toss it. Destroy the social security card, too," Mr. Forrester said. "I'd like the family pictures back. I'd appreciate having those. On second thought, save all of it for me. Can I come by this afternoon? Where do you live?"

"Oh, I forgot. I really wasn't thinking. Sunnyvale Public Safety said they'd pick up the things and get them to you next week."

"Just tell me where you live. I'll get right over there."

Cynthia's neck stiffened. She caught her breath, tried to remember if she'd given her name. "I'm sorry. I prefer to hand everything over to the police. There are at least two people's cards here."

The man slammed down his phone. He took a deep breath. He had her number, with a few taps of his computer keys, he had her name, address, political contributions, place of birth. Could have been much worse than a housewife. It still irritated him that he'd lost his wallet. Homeland Security agents are supposed to be immune.

* * *

Cynthia looked at her friends in the clubhouse. A shadow passed over her face. "I guess I never told you that the man whose wallet I found was a Homeland Security agent."

She resumed reading her manuscript, but she noticed her friends' shock. They sat straighter, little frowns crumpled foreheads. Sue brought her hand to her chest, then pulled it away with her other hand. The meaning of the words on the folders Cynthia had placed in front of the women leaped from the page.

Chapter 7

March 19, 2004

Madison slept well most of the night before their departure for Kona. Deep in REM sleep, she lay on her back and dreamed. The goddess intervened with a warning, a message of understanding rather than avoidance. There could be no avoidance, but understanding would help. She chose a form Madison could recognize, the Goddess Pele at Red Hill.

Fishermen knew the coastal landmark south of Kailua-Kona but before Kealakekua. Madison dreamed of sunshine sparkles on blue water. She and Ev fished off Red Hill closer to shore than usual at about sixty fathoms. Madison studied the shoreline.

"I see it! Ev, look! The eyes. I've never recognized the eyes before."

"Where?"

"See the red color with the dark layers, the openings? It's the 'face' Paul Gouveia told us about."

"Looks more like a skull to me."

"Pele's eyes, or a skull. A warning either way. That's what Paul said. When part of the island fell into the sea, those lava tubes were exposed. Now I understand. The iron red color, Pele's color and the color of blood. Her eyes watching. What was the third thing? He said the ancient Hawaiians avoided this place, called it Pu'u Ohau, Pathway to the Heavens or Halfway to the Heavens. There was something else."

"The rock. The rock that floats."

"That's it, Ev. The light, frothy, extra porous lava that floats on water for a little while. Paul said all those things together caused the ancients to avoid this place. They feared and revered the area."

Ev watched black clouds tumble over Hualalai's summit and pointed. "Squall coming, honey."

Madison looked up, then back at Red Hill. She saw the skull now, not Pele's face.

"Looks like a bad one," Ev said. "We're going to get wet."

The clouds enfolded their boat and blotted out the world.

Madison awoke, wet with perspiration. In the darkness she rolled her lips into her mouth and brought her fingertips together. Her thoughts tumbled against each other. Sleep didn't return.

Chapter 8

March 20, 2004

Airport security swept the crowded passenger concourse at Oakland International Airport at 8:20 AM. A German Shepherd and his handler moved fast, startling people. Marie Angles worked quickly, changing the trash can liners in the food concession areas. She didn't see the dog.

Evert and Madison Druid sat in a tiny food court area and ate breakfast burritos. They knew from experience to check in early, especially today with Madison's sprained right knee and the big, ugly brace over her tan jeans. Experience also taught them the hearty airport burritos were excellent. They saw a blur.

The dog darted by and goosed the janitor. Marie shot up with a full bag of garbage. The plastic bag split and spewed garbage over the Druid's table. As if in silent slow motion, an industrial-sized coffee filter of soggy grounds landed on Madison's blouse and tumbled into her lap.

"Shit," said Madison. Marie, the janitor, said something equivalent, but Madison's Spanish class hadn't covered those words.

Madison stood and brushed off her clothes. "Good thing I wore a dark blouse."

"Your pants are going to be a problem," said Ev. Madison frowned at him while she pulled bits of the shredded coffee filter from her knee brace.

"Sorry, honey." Ev tried to help. "I'm sure they will replace our breakfast."

"I've finished breakfast! I'm going to clean up." She grabbed her splattered carry-on and headed for the Women's room. She slowed her pace when she saw the line. It curved out the entrance well into Gate 10's waiting area.

It took seventeen minutes to reach a stall, a cramped one with little room for her carry-on bag. "I'll watch it for you," said a woman in a denim jacket and faded jeans. "I saw what happened."

"Thank you. This brace makes things difficult enough. No one would try anything with so many people around watching."

Another woman took over guarding Madison's carry-on when a stall opened for the first one. Madison emerged to find an unsmiling woman in a black pants suit standing over her carry-on. "Not a good idea," said the woman when Madison thanked her.

At a small sink, Madison used a dampened paper towel to clean off her knee brace and carry-on. The large, paper napkin she had in her lap at breakfast deflected the bulk of the coffee grounds. The stains could have been worse.

Chapter 9

March 20, 2004

On the Kona Coast of the Big Island, the surf rose and caught the forecasters by surprise. Waves moved with the speed of a sudden squall. They crashed into ancient lava flows along the shore and exploded white foam hundreds of feet into the air. On Hualalai's summit, a goddess drew in the vaporized sea spray and breathed it out again.

"Could be an undersea landslide," said *Kakui's* captain when the Coast Guard cutter radioed headquarters in Honolulu. "We can't explain it. No known cause, sir. Not at this time."

"All things have causes," whispered the Trades. The goddess nodded. Coconut palms quivered agreement and waved their fronds in a hula of farewell. Pele caught the Trades' message. Hawaiians noticed her breathing quicken. Little crevasses open to the air and lined with traces of moist, yellow sulfur felt her breath hotter than usual. Even from Hualalai, the volcano guarding Kona,

Pele breathed the hot breath of impatience through thousands of tubes, large and small.

* * *

In Oakland, California, Madison and Evert Druid stood in line for the direct Aloha Airlines flight to Kona. Several other retired couples, some young adults and a few families with small children waited.

"Doesn't look like a full flight," Madison said and shifted her hibiscus print shoulder bag in front of her trying to hide the coffee stains.

"That's good," said Ev. They had their photo identification ready, but the joking, friendly Hawaiian behind the counter lost his smile. Sweat broke out on his forehead when he took their driver's licenses. The other ticket agents glanced up and edged away, eyes hooded. The man punched a single key on his computer.

"Sorry, sir." He swallowed and looked down. His voice hushed. "They wanted I.D. confirmation. They've been waiting. Sorry."

"Problem?" Evert could tell there was. Madison saw the woman from the restroom and three men in dark business suits rush at them. So did Ev.

"Mr. and Mrs. Druid, you are wanted for questioning under authority of the Patriot Act. Come with us." The closest agent spun Evert around, no easy task because Ev stood six feet five to the agent's five nine. Someone spun Madison around too, but the momentum continued her spin. Her knee brace caught an agent hard, behind his knee, and he stumbled.

Madison swiped at the air in front of her face, as if brushing way a pesky fly. "Tell someone! We're Madison and Ev Druid. Tell someone!" Gray hair flying, coffee stains and all, Madison lost it.

"Come quietly. Do not resist."

Madison screamed. Arms flailing, she appealed to the ticket agent, to the startled people in line. "Tell someone. Tell everyone! Maddy and Evert Druid. Remember us. Evert and Madison Druid!"

"What's going on?" Someone called from the line of passengers.

"No comment. Step back. Do not interfere. No comment." The agents took Madison and Ev firmly by both arms and pulled them away. Ev said, "It's a mistake, honey. We'll get it ironed out."

Madison continued to scream. "Druid! Evert and Madison. From Auburn. Los Altos before that. Tell someone! Help us!"

A young man in line stepped forward. "What's this all about? What'd they do? Who are they? Who are you?"

"Department of Homeland Security. Are you with them?"

"No!" His arms up in surrender, he said, "Just wonder…"

He received a glare and a hard shove. "Do not interfere."

Ev and Madison stood together in front of the terminal, hemmed in by security officers. People stared. Ev searched his wife's face. "Maddy, you okay?"

"Fine, darling. No more screaming. I promise." She paused, attempted a smile. "The face from Red Hill. The skull. Like a last warning. I saw it floating over the ticket counter. I love you, Ev. Forever."

Ev leaned closer. "I love you, Maddy. Always."

An agent pulled him away. "Very touching. Mr. Druid, step into the car, please. Mrs. Druid, over there." The agent indicated the second car for Madison and braced himself for another outburst that didn't come.

Overhead, a brazen, white and gray seagull swallowed a moldy tuna sandwich crust purloined from a distant garbage can. The gull wiped his beak on the metal edge of the pedestrian signal that flashed DON'T WALK. Startled by the commotion and abrupt squeal of tires as the first car pulled away, the bird deposited an explosion of colorful shit on the second car's windshield.

Chapter 10

Randy Salazar was a stringer for the *Oakland Tribune*. He'd talked to the Druids about fishing in Kona while they'd waited in line.

"Didn't look like terrorists to me," he said to the ticket agent after things calmed down.

"Same here. Those federal guys were real jerks." He looked up suddenly. "Ah, that's just between us. Okay, brah?"

"That's cool."

Upgraded to First Class, the *Trib* reporter stopped at a pay phone and called in his story, dictated on the spot. The man searching the phone book in the next booth heard Randy's side of the conversation.

"Yeah, Auburn and Los Altos. I'm sure someone can run them down in the database. Find people who know them."

"Ah, how about Rodney or Arlene?"

"But wait. Wait! I got upgraded to First Class! Lots of people saw them."

Randy pinched his forehead, rubbed his hand back and forth over his jaw. "And my girlfriend."

"Well, I'll have a girlfriend by then, and we'll want to fly First Class."

"Yeah, okay. Ask Terry to do the Internet search. I'll drive to Los Altos from here. Keep your fingers crossed."

Randy Salazar caught the shuttle to the long-term lot where he'd left his beat-up Honda Civic coupe and thumbed in a call to the office. "Need the numbers for the local papers in Auburn and Los Altos, Arlene. How 'bout the *San Jose Mercury News*, too."

While he waited at a red before driving onto the Nimitz Freeway heading south, he started calling. The *Auburn Journal* yielded little information, but he left his cell number. The *Towne Crier* line was busy. He gave up on the phone and drove.

The *Crier* editor was in a meeting. Ms. Sydney Minamoto, a feature writer, asked if she could help. The elegant Ms. Minamoto had black hair and bangs. Randy wondered how old she was. He guessed somewhere between forty-nine and fifty-nine. He didn't know why, but he felt a little like he had when he was eight, the time his mom caught him tying his little brother to a tree. Serious dark eyes studied Randy when he explained what information he needed.

"Madison and Ev Druid are friends of mine. They live in Auburn. Just a moment. I'd better call the *Tribune*."

"Sure. Number's on my card." Randy whipped out his card. Sydney Minamoto took his card but said, "I have the number."

Through a glass partition, Randy watched her run a manicured red nail down a sheet of paper taped to the wall as she picked up the receiver. She returned still serious. No smile. She asked for his driver's license, studied it and relaxed. "May I record our conversation? I sense a story, too. Let's start over. Why do you want information about the Druids?"

Randy bit his lip. This was not how he envisioned the meeting. He liked to ask the questions.

When Randy finished, Sydney said, "It's a mistake. Maybe we're talking about a different couple with the same name." Little creases appeared around her eyes and between her brows.

Randy watched her. "If you know them, you know they go to Hawaii often. Have a fishing boat. You know that, don't you?"

"Something's wrong. Very wrong. They lived here in town for years. Like thirty. Our kids grew up together. I asked Madison to introduce me when I received the Citizen of the Year Award. She's the one I asked. Do you understand what I'm saying?" She stared at Randy.

"Evert was on the city council. They were PTA presidents, active in soccer and in the schools. They supported Music in the Schools and the San Jose Taiko. Madison taught at the high school and at San Jose State University."

"Who else should I see? Others here in town?"

"Sure. I'll give you a list. Everyone's in the phone book. I have a deadline, but I could make some calls tonight."

"You won't put out the story yet? I mean it's… I'm the one… They were arrested right in front of me. I want to get to the bottom of things. The story breaks tomorrow with as much follow-up as I can get over the next two days. Do you have file photos I can use?"

"Yes, I took most of them. I'll pull them for you. Credit to the *Crier* and to the photographer, of course?"

"Of course."

"Promise me you'll be fair." Sydney held him with her eyes. "Be fair, whatever happens. Are you a brave man, Randy Salazar?"

The question caught Randy unprepared. He stared back, moving his lips silently. At last, he said, "As brave as the next person, I guess."

"We'll see, Randy Salazar. We'll see."

Chapter 11

CITIZENS ARRESTED

FBI and Homeland Security Make Arrests in Every State

Civil Liberties Groups Caught by Surprise

The headline ran above Randy's story the next morning, with additional details from the national wire services. The Associated Press connected the dots from many such stories across the country. Randy's follow up stories needed depth, answers to Why? What? Where? When? All anyone had was the Who.

He met the Forest Vista Tennis and Philosophy group gathered at the neighborhood club the following morning. Cynthia opened the locked heavy wooden gate when he knocked.

"You look tired," she said even though she'd never met him.

"Didn't get much sleep last night." He joined the four women around an outdoor table with an umbrella that left his seat in the sun. They had seen the headlines, the newscasts. No one else was around.

Randy faced intense expressions, worry. He asked to record their conversation. Cynthia's eyes checked around the table without moving her head. "That's okay, I guess."

"If you stop when we want to go off the record. You turn it off if we ask you to," said Peach.

"Peach, that your real name?"

"Oralee. Her name's Oralee White," said Kate.

Peach used the voice she saved for classroom discipline. Her left hand moved to her hip. "Use anything but Peach, and I'll sue. You and your paper." Her friends grinned and gave the lie to her threat. Her voice softened. "I go by Peach White."

"Fine." Randy clicked his tiny recorder, pulled out his pen and his questions. "Names?"

He repeated Cynthia Fields, Kate Yoshihara, Sue Riddle and Peach White as he wrote. He turned back to his questions, but Cynthia began first.

"It's a mistake, of course. Some horrible mistake. Where are they? We've made a few calls. Oakland police say they don't know. San Francisco police have no clue. NAS Alameda won't talk to us. Kate has a call in to the governor's office. The FBI wouldn't talk to Sue. What have you uncovered?"

"I... I... Nothing definite. A few rumors about a military flight overseas. Out of Travis. Couple people mentioned Subic Bay, off the record. Looks like we have a collection of activists from around the country. Odd that the Druids are political unknowns in Auburn.

If they were activists, it was here in Los Altos and Santa Clara County."

"Think about it," said Peach. "It's not as disruptive to turn in someone who's moved away than to nail a current community leader. That's what it looks like, doesn't it? Community leaders. The ones who oppose the war in Iraq?"

"Peach has a blunt side," said Sue with a weak smile for Randy and a quick warning glare at Peach.

"Turn in? What do you mean by 'turn in'?" Randy fixed his attention on Peach.

Cynthia nudged a foot against Peach's foot, but said, "Turn in?" as if thinking aloud.

Kate said, "We're off the record here," and pointed to the tape recorder. Randy nodded but didn't turn off the recorder.

"Think about it," Peach said. "Unless we're way more technologically advanced than I realized, our government has picked up ordinary citizens who happen to oppose, or are likely to oppose, the war. No, let's narrow it. Let's say those who oppose the administration. Those 'ungodly ones' who oppose the President."

"Peach, you're going too far," said Sue.

Peach ignored her and continued her brainstorming. "Where do they get the names? Ideally, from local leaders who support the war. But that turns into an instant witch hunt, a convenient way to eliminate opposition on all kinds of local fronts."

Sue nibbled her thumbnail. "So here in town we have a smarter than average person who sees a chance to save the community some strife by naming someone who no longer lives here."

"Maybe so," said Peach and ran her finger over her lower lip.

"Who?" Kate wanted to know. Then to Randy, "Promise we're off the record."

"I promise." But he still didn't turn off the recorder. Kate narrowed her eyes and dropped her chin. Randy said, "I'll fax an advance copy to you before it goes to press."

"Who?" Kate asked again. "Who would turn in the Druids, of all people?"

"Doesn't matter now," said Cynthia. "Who turned them in is a distracting tangent."

"Right," said Peach. "We need to know where Maddy and Evert are and get them out. Or, at least find out why they're detained. What are the charges? What does 'person of interest' mean?"

Kate turned to Randy. "What else have you learned?"

"Sydney Miramoto's a good source. Seems to know everyone and everything. She didn't want to talk to me at first. We worked it out. I used one of her photos. My story ran on the front page of today's *Tribune*. She's doing a follow up for the *Crier* Wednesday."

"Any reason there's no one we know about from San Francisco, or Oakland or Berkeley, for that matter?" Peach continued thinking aloud.

"My editor noticed that, too. He thinks there's no way to quiet those cities anyhow. Maybe the fear from the surrounding communities will infect them over time. Or, maybe we haven't found everyone who was picked up."

A moment passed, then Kate asked what else Randy learned.

"Here in town, to be honest, the only negative thing I've turned up is a comment by the wife of an ex-mayor who served on the city council years before Evert Druid served." The women waited. "Her only comment was that Madison struck her as being somewhat aloof."

The three women spoke at once.

"Ha!"

"Outrageous!"

"Who is this ex-mayor's wife we're talking about here?" Cynthia looked to her friends for confirmation. "Looks like we might have our tattletale."

Sue counseled calm with a tilt of head and a raised hand.

"You just looking for negative things?" Kate's mask of stone made Randy shiver despite the bright sunshine blinding him.

The garden service truck arrived, and the crew entered with their noisy blower and mower even though Los Altos has an ordinance that limits blower noise. Cynthia unlocked the clubhouse, and they moved inside to escape the racket.

"I've found only positive things," said Randy. "Those who've agreed to talk to me about the Druids display shock, outrage, like you. They don't understand it. People even liked their kids. Half the Homestead senior class lined up to shake Madison Druid's hand each time one of their kids graduated."

"Yeah. They were very involved in the schools," Cynthia said and nodded. "Not only city council and committees."

"They supported music in the community as well. The independent Mountain View School of Music and the Arts, and the Palo Alto Community Arts Center," Kate said. "And, they supported me." She stuck her index finger under one lens of her sunglasses she continued to wear inside. She rubbed her eye then pinched her nose.

"How so?" Randy jotted on his notes.

Kate moved both index fingers to her eyes, propped her elbows on the table and drew a deep breath. "This is scary."

After a pause, Cynthia said, "Kate's a concert pianist. She teaches advanced students by audition only." She indicated the other three with her hand. "We attend her concerts, prepare the food. We help each other. All any one of us has to do is call the others and someone will be there. We do what we can for each other. Should one of us have a problem, the rest help out. See? Maddy was one of us. We know each other very well."

"She was the heart of our group," Kate said and again her eyes misted.

"It could be a problem with the group at church or as major as a life-threatening illness. We're friends." Peach curled her hand over her mouth. Her eyes reddened too, then the tip of her nose.

Randy absorbed the silent consensus. "Is it fair to say you were her closest friends?"

Cynthia's shoulders went up and down. "Maddy and Evert had lots of close friends. Couldn't have run for office if they hadn't. Lots of people devoted all kinds of effort and time to their campaigns and their causes."

"We are among her closest friends, but she has others," said Kate. "Here in town, I'd say Sydney Miramoto, Barb Fjeld, Leslie English, Ed and Jean Rower, lots of tennis friends and then the people who've moved away, like the Sandovals, the Johnsons, the LeBlancs. Don't know if Madison still keeps in touch with them or not."

"You do know Maddy's parents lived in Los Altos Hills?" said Peach. "They're both dead now, but they had a wide range of friends and contacts, especially in tennis and retired military circles."

"Yes, Eunice, her mom, was a great lady, nationally ranked in women's doubles in the 75's and 80's age groups," said Kate. "She inspired all of us." Heads nodded.

"Ex-military? Her parents? Tell me about that," said Randy.

"Maddy's dad was a career Navy officer," said Cynthia. She spoke with unusual enthusiasm, eager to highlight Ev and Madison's military connection. "World War II veteran, Korea. Madison lived all over when she was a kid. Evert was a Naval officer, too, right out of college, then returned to civilian life. He was an engineering manager before he retired."

"Vietnam?" asked Randy.

"Think Ev's service was just before we got involved in a big way. Maddy's brothers served in Vietnam."

Peach said, "Madison and Ev were good at putting together teams, groups of people for different causes."

Randy paged through his notes. "Appears the union reps were okay with Evert, too. Will Sledge told me he respected Evert in spite of sometimes acrimonious negotiations.

"Any of you know Madison in college? At Cal?"

Kate reacted. Her straight posture became rigid. "Going kinda far back. Not one of those anti-Berkeley people, are you?"

"I'm a Cal grad! Majored in journalism," said Randy. "Just wondered if any of you knew her back then."

Sue put her elbow on the table, her chin in her hand and her index finger over her mouth while she followed the verbal Ping-Pong.

"Ev went to Stanford," said Kate. "You talk to anyone who went to school with him?"

"Yeah, couple fraternity brothers, a guy who rowed crew with him in the freshman boat. Also found a division president at HP living in Idaho who worked with him when they both started out. Couldn't trace down any Navy contacts yet, from his service years. Seems like they're model citizens, both of them. But…" Randy looked at each woman. "I was surprised to learn they were registered Republicans when they lived here, that's all. Evert Druid still is. Madison switched to the Democrats like lots of people in the mid-nineties." He waited but received no response from the women.

"Look," he said. "She graduated in the '60's. Not exactly a calm, quiet time at Berkeley."

"So did I." Kate folded her arms. "I didn't really know Madison at Cal. We lived on campus, in the same dorm her senior year. I was a junior. Lived on the eighth floor. Don't know which floor she was on. We confirmed our Cal connection when we became neighbors here. Your assumptions are wrong. All kinds of people attend Cal, all political philosophies and stripes.

"The one time I remember Madison was a gathering when Harry Bridges spoke at the dorm complex where we lived. Maddy and a few others asked questions, challenged him." Kate saw blank looks around her. "Harry Bridges, the Communist leader of the Longshoremen's Union back then, or something like that. Anyway, Maddy said it was not enough to criticize and discard a government without examining the system proposed for its replacement. She didn't think highly of his proposals. I remember thinking she was either stupid or brave to expose herself to the jeers from some in the crowd. I kept my thoughts to myself in those days.

"Look, all I'm saying is attending Cal in the '60's doesn't mean a person is a radical of some kind or other. I was a Republican then. I'm a Republican now."

Peach said, "Understandable, given your family history during World War II."

"Peach, I think for myself." Kate's words had a deliberate slowness.

Peach pressed her lips, looked down and then up with a shrug. The reporter turned back to his prepared questions. Near the end, he sprung his one trap.

"Tell me what you know about the protest march in '96."

Three blank faces answered him. Sue said in disbelief, "Oh please. A protest march in 1996?"

Cynthia's right eyebrow bounced once. She glanced down at the table and began without preamble. "She asked me if I wanted to go. Guess it was '96. It was years ago. I declined. Wish I'd gone, sometimes. I'm not the marching type. It was a 'fight the right' march for women's rights."

"No guts," Peach said. She caught Cynthia's sharp look and added, "Course I didn't go either. Maddy didn't mention it."

"Nothing wrong with a peaceful march. Free speech and all." Kate turned to Cynthia. "She went by herself? Where was it? San Jose? San Francisco?"

"The City. Yes. Told me she had to go," said Cynthia. "She went by herself. Later, she wrote about the experience. That's how I know she went. The police took pictures of the marchers. That can't be what this is about?" Color crept up Cynthia's neck. Pink blotches grew on her cheeks. "There were no arrests." Her voice rose. "A completely peaceful march. Moms and little kids, all kinds of people marched, apparently. The papers covered it." Cynthia looked around for confirmation. Again, blank stares.

"Still have it?" Randy asked. "What she wrote?"

"Maybe."

"Could I make a copy?"

"If I can find it. Sure." Cynthia grimaced.

In the parking lot, as they left, Peach heard Cynthia mumble, "What's happening to our country? I don't recognize it anymore."

"We get the government we deserve," Peach said. "Ultimately, we're responsible for the actions of our government."

Cynthia gave her a puzzled look and sighed. "That doesn't make me feel better. I'm frightened, Peach. Maybe we shouldn't talk any more. We could be arrested too."

Peach walked to her car. "If truth is the first casualty of war, then silence is its shroud."

Chapter 12

Ev and Madison's Memorial

Forest Vista, March 2006

"I gave each of you copies of Madison's story of the 1996 protest march when that reporter from the *Tribune*, Randy Salazar, first came down here. I included it in here since you felt it might be part of the puzzle.

"Sue, would you read it, please. It'll give me a little break."

Sue stood without a word. She took Cynthia's spiral-bound manuscript and read aloud Madison's story of the protest demonstration.

A March in Two Voices
April 14, 1996

The *San Francisco Chronicle* news editor assigned reporter Rita Nile to cover the demonstration. He told her to include individual motivation. "What was it that brings these thousands here? They look normal, polite. Women, men, young and old, all races, mothers with small children. Find out why they came."

For one or two in garish costume, motivation was obvious. *I won't interview the publicity-seekers.* She mixed with the crowd and composed her story for her benignly skeptical editor, who nonetheless cut just one paragraph from the bottom and ran it the next day. But I think she missed important parts of the story. When I heard her interviewing someone, I knew she'd miss my story and Pua's.

Madison's Voice

They act like young adolescents at a circus freak show. They've pulled their bicycles right into the barricades on Marina Boulevard, the two women bracketed by the two men who talk over them, out of the sides of their mouths while they stare into the crowd of marchers. Only the men talk. The homes of some of San Francisco's wealthiest inhabitants line the boulevard. Those who live on the front row of the Marina district have unobstructed views across Marina Green and the yacht harbor to San Francisco Bay, the Golden Gate Bridge and Treasure Island. The two couples have not come far. Perhaps they did not know about the National Organization of Women's march this warm Sunday. We march in opposition to the extreme Right agenda. Perhaps these four read only the financial pages. Maybe they merely wanted a pleasant bike ride round the green and found their way blocked by thousands of marchers. Since they show no anger, they probably think they appear neutral. They don't.

I feel their detached disdain, especially from the men. Discrete nudges, a slight movement of an index finger. They probably see no one like themselves, even when such people march by them. They seem to seek the differences, the more extreme, the better. They stare. Their eyes search for the bizarre and validation for not marching themselves.

The couples have the look of young professionals. The men wear their hair cut short, but not military short. The women wear oxford cloth blouses with their tailored shorts, buttoned-down white shirts and tailored shorts for the men. No helmets or riding gloves or the attire of serious bikers. They wanted a simple ride, probably just a few blocks from home.

The dignitaries at the front of our serpentine column reach Crissy Field and wait to address the rally when we all arrive. It's a long wait, and Gloria Steinem has a plane to catch. We delight in the huge turnout, even though it causes delays. Gloria's given us her name and presence. That's enough. She heads back to the starting point, returning down the long march route, outside the barricades. The couples with bicycles do not turn or recognize the elegant woman, the protestor on their side of the barriers. Gloria wears casual black clothes that contrast with her distinctive blond hair. She has her trademark sunglasses and moves with a model's grace. Gloria acknowledges our greetings and waves, but we do not use her last name. If we had, the four people at the barricades might have turned and seen her.

Maybe they notice the "Angry White Guys for Affirmative Action," but then, that group is on my side of the barricades, and the four must see their banner. If these onlookers are attorneys, they notice the Asian Law Students Association. One of the bicycle women is Asian, and the law students pass right in front of the four before I do. Maybe they are accountants, or bankers, or stock brokers.

I hope they see my big diamond wedding ring, my tailored white blouse, expensive sunglasses, my gray hair, the red sash that says I am one of the NOW volunteers who take the official march count of the day. Would it surprise them to know that I am still a registered Republican, even if I don't vote that way?

I considered not attending. It would have been easier not to take this Sunday out of my comfortable life. Paying dues and occasionally volunteering for office work is different than marching on a Sunday afternoon. Easy indeed not to pull my husband home early from a weekend at the lake so I can be here. But I'm here.

The state Supreme Court's ruling this spring, further restricting women's rights, told me I needed to be here. Everyone who values freedom needs to be here. I don't like the restrictions some religious groups and others would codify to narrow our pluralistic society. I came alone. I can do more than discuss issues with my friends and have interesting cocktail conversations about current events.

We round a curve and squeeze down to funnel through the cyclone-fencing gate into Crissy Field.

A policeman stands on a platform and rapidly snaps pictures of the crowd. He carefully frames each segment of the marchers while we slowly move through the narrow opening.

"They're taking our pictures! If they want to send us to showers inside, there's going to be trouble," says a man to my right.

A news helicopter circles the rally site, a few small planes pass overhead, too, but the helicopter circles and circles. My job was from ten until two. It's now past three and the volunteer tent calls for more volunteers. I need to get off my feet for a few minutes. I catch a few words from Patricia Ireland and Jesse Jackson. Can't see them from this distance. It's hard to hear much with the helicopter overhead, but I stay far back from the stage where I found a small patch of ground to sit with less chance of being trampled. I think of the two couples.

I could be wrong. I, too, stood by once in 1958, in Athens, Georgia. There was no sound in the ordinary sense, only the quiet authority of hundreds and hundreds of people. The marchers appeared unexpectedly, filling Lumpkin Street and spilling across the sidewalks and lawns along the way. They headed past the University, toward downtown. No chanting, singing, no sixties finger cymbals or bongo drum beats, no identifying banners. Black men and women, old and young, marched silently like a wave washing the land then gone. I see their quiet majesty clearly again today.

So maybe I'm wrong about the two couples. Perhaps one of the women, or one of the men, will store away an impression of today, an impression that will not leave them, one that will encourage her or him to think about the good of us all.

Pua's Voice

It's hot. Glad I wore my cutoffs and enlarged the armholes in this sweatshirt when I cut the sleeves out. Good to have my arms free. Can't stand being all fettered in straps and elastic. No bra for me. I'm not wearing that red sash either. It'll get in the way. The Peace armband's okay, I guess.

It's great, really good, all these organizations here. More than six hundred thirty groups, they say. Of course, the cops and park service people aren't too thrilled. Never are with big gatherings. Those park service guys on their horses look like statues sitting there in the saddle with their creased shirts and Smokey Bear hats. I see two, but there might be four, mounted up, for show. That one on the knoll, deliberately poised for effect, does he think he scares us? The big, bay Morgans are good-looking animals, though. I give 'em that. The gelding stands probably more than fifteen hands. I'm not here to watch horses.

I'll keep my eyes on the crowd. Peaceful as a picnic. Don't see any skinheads around, but you never know. Better get down to help with the crowd control training, since Mollie and Alice expect me. Glad we decided to run through the training right here, before we head out.

Alice should use a cordless mike for these sessions. Her voice squeaks. This bunch doesn't look like they need the non-violent, non-confrontational pep talk. Some of this group would have a hard time facing down a store clerk who cheated them. That's all right. That's all right. Glad you came. It's good that they understand how the police don't care how an incident starts. You tell 'em, Alice. Police will arrest anyone around. And don't we know it. Oh-oh, Alice spotted me.

"Pua. Trina. Anyone else here had self-defense training? I need some volunteers to demonstrate what I've been talking about, how to isolate a troublemaker. I need a troublemaker. Okay, you. Get into an angry confrontation with her. Okay, Pua, Trina, you others, link arms!"

We link arms. Alice's voice cracks. "You want your backs to the person you're isolating, except for one person who positions herself right in front of the troublemaker and tries to calm that person. Now watch the others move."

Works perfectly. Circle the racist hatemonger, or the jerk, or whomever, and move him off, away. Of course, he'd fight harder than this little thing. Wonder if someone will try anything today. Don't want trouble, but I'm ready. Lots of kids, little guys in strollers, moms and daughters. Need to keep 'em safe. I see you kids. I'll do my best.

I'll walk close as I can to the side, right along the barricades. If there's going to be trouble, most likely it'll come on the edges. God, it's hot with all these people. Where's the breeze off the bay?

Ah, finally a breath of air, not much, but it should pick up. Here we go. It's taken long enough. The leaders could be at Crissy Field by now. No trouble so far. We aren't expecting any, but then we weren't expecting to have those twenty-six Port-a-Potties torched last night either.

Oh, oh. Those two bozos look nasty. Big, especially that one coming over the barrier with his red NOW sign. Unhappy and in a hurry. They join us but move faster, passing people like germs in the blood stream. Trina's close. Who else?

"Trina, I don't like the looks of those two."

"I see them."

With the flow, we start across an intersection. The whole group moves faster. I don't know which street it is. Don't care. The two football types wave their signs and watch the intersection. They want people to see them. Trina and I move closer. We pick up Pete and a big Mexican guy. Behind us, the American Association of University Women, middle-aged types, have discreetly slowed down in front of two families with kids in strollers, keeping them back, all of us work together without any more than my call to Trina and Pete and a nod toward our "friends". What great heads-up cooperation. We're ready if there's a problem.

"There they go." Pete's hand indicates their direction.

Through the intersection and past a couple of houses into the next block, the men toss their signs, jump the barriers again. They walk away fast. They don't look back. I shake my head at Pete. "Some kind of childish prank."

"Maybe they lost a bet." Pete gives me a clenched fist sign and a smile.

"Thanks, guys."

"De nada."

"When's Randy getting' back from Hawaii, Pua? He owes me a few beers."

"Tomorrow night, Pete. Don't you tell him I asked for help. It'll spoil my image."

He laughs. "You didn't need no help. Those guys ran when they saw you comin'."

At Crissy Field that cop standing on top of the van, he's taking pictures. Quiet crowd. No sign of trouble anywhere, and some cop takes pictures. Ignore him. The AAUW women look insulted, probably hasn't happened to them before.

I smile at the women. "Thanks for your help back there." They smile back, tell me I'm welcome. My appearance might have put them off at first, but they're real chatty now. That's what it's all about, reaching out to everyone, work together. What I'd like to know is how do we build understanding with those who want to stop us, kill us, or take pictures of us?

* * *

After the speeches, shuttle buses take the marchers back to the foot of Mission, across from the Ferry Building, to the Bay Area Rapid Transit connection.

Madison and Pua board the same BART car. Pua spots Madison's NOW button: Elect Women for a Change.

"You at the march?" Pua asks.

"Of course," Madison says and returns Pua's thumbs-up sign. "I saw you during the peace-keeping demonstration. No trouble today, was there?"

"Not during the march. A church social." Pua doesn't mention the incident she witnessed or the Port-a-Potties. Great turnout, they agree. Pua thinks the march could impact the June election.

"If not June, maybe November, and the midterm election in 1998," Madison says. "Momentum's growing."

* * *

The reporter phoned in her story and didn't wait for a shuttle. She'd watched the marchers assemble then dashed ahead to Crissy Field for some quotes from the celebrities. The police framed her in one of their pictures even though she waved her press pass. The next day her byline ran on page one, under the photo of the leaders at the step-off point. A straight news piece. Sixty thousand the police estimated. Closer to eighty said NOW and produced the march count signatures. The story said nothing about what motivated the people who marched. When she reviewed it, did the reporter think she should have asked better follow-up questions, talked to more individuals? Perhaps the big woman who took part in the training session at the assembly

Linda Lanterman

point or one of the sixty-year-olds. Or a teenager, or a young mother.

Chapter 13

Philippine Islands

March 2004

Leonard "Law" Hayhill, Operations Director for Across the Board Contractors, scouted the Olongapo site weeks before it's official designation by the United States and the Philippines. The retired Special Forces Officer guessed correctly that it would be selected for the detention facility. The company paid him for his educated guesses. He rarely missed. He rested his elbow on his standup desk in his one room office and talked with one of his employees from Oahu.

"You related? Know him before now?"

"No, boss. He's from da Big Island, Kona side."

"Okay, tell me more."

"He's a US citizen, speaks Tagalog, big Hawaiian guy."

"Bigger than you?"

"Maybe 'bout da same. Da kine. You know."

"What kind? English, Don."

"Da kine you want with you in a dark alley. No one mess with him. Has a Filipina wife, couple kids. Lives up mauka. Has a little house, planted coffee himself, 'bout one hundred trees. Has idea about bringing gourmet coffee to the Philippines. His partner and him own a machine shop downtown, but he say the coffee's all junk this year. Too much rain. And not too much money from the machine shop. He needs work for cash."

"Can he be trusted?"

"Sure, boss. Runs a clean operation. No bad scuttlebutt, but if he gives you stinkeye, you want your gun close. For sura." The man laughed.

"Okay. Get the paperwork going. Have him come in tomorrow. What's his name?"

"Hutch Okakope, boss."

Chapter 14

California Bay Area, March 2004

Madison saw Ev while they were on a military bus. Four buses departed into the night before the last of the men and then the women filed up to the remaining buses. The men occupied the front, women the back, detainees in every other row. Ev and Madison exchanged secret smiles, tiny winks, a touch. Ev gave her a reassuring nudge with his elbow as she passed his seatback when she moved down the aisle. They dared not speak. Too many guards. The bus headed north from NAS Alameda up the freeway, across the Carquinez Straight to Highway 80. Ev and Madison knew the route and would have guessed Travis Air Force Base was their destination. They guessed right.

Their bus drove directly onto the tarmac. The MPs unshackled the men and lined them up outside. A C-130 waited, hatch open. The bus driver slid into his seat and started the ignition. Ev and a couple others looked back at the bus. He couldn't see inside the windows where Madison sat, but he raised his head in a quick nod and tried to smile. A tear ran down Madison's face, but she straightened and watched Ev until the bus raced away.

* * *

The goddess' laugh tumbled among the clouds on sea breezes pushing inland. The same breezes that carried the military orders also collected the countermanded orders, the confused communications and the angry growls of officers.

"Two planes! Put 'em all on the C-130 with a few extra MPs. There's plenty of room."

"But we're fueled up, sir. Ready."

"One plane. That's the word from the High Command. Bless 'em."

* * *

Madison clung to the feeble hope that Ev and she might be flown on the same plane. The women, still in the buses, waited inside a hanger for ten minutes. It seemed like an hour. When the driver returned this time, he drove back to the plane the men had boarded. "Thank you" swam in Madison's head. Thank you. Thank you. Her small happiness lasted until the plane taxied to the runway for takeoff.

"Good morning, ladies and gentlemen." Sarcasm dripped from the captain's voice over the intercom. "You best settle in for a long flight. I'm not permitted to tell you how long. I advise you to obey your flight attendants and make no fuss. Should you annoy our flight attendants, we have special restraint compartments for your use." He chuckled. "These compartments are much less comfortable than your seats.

"We are aboard a Lockheed C-130 Hercules, four-engine turboprop. It's a good plane for short field landings but much slower than the newer planes. For your safety, we have securely fastened you to your seats." He laughed and clicked off.

The woman sitting closest to Madison stuck out the tip of her tongue and grimaced. "Yeah, unprofessional," whispered Madison as she tried to ignore the shackles and the complaints of her right knee. At least the uncomfortable brace was gone. It was tossed with other personal possessions in a pile at NAS Alameda. Madison had doubts about the brace, but she'd promised her doctor she would wear it. Now she couldn't.

* * *

Four of the guards on their flight were women, small comfort. They shoved and swore and called the detainees "scum". Madison told time by timing the different shifts. They flew into the night. They landed somewhere and took off. Madison thought it was day, then night and day again, but she didn't know for sure. The detainees could not see outside. At least they must have felt lucky about the absence of the prisoners' hoods they'd seen on television.

Every several hours the guards permitted a bathroom break, a few detainees at a time. A woman named Paz begged to use the restroom. Those near her heard the high note in her request. Two or three took up her cause.

"Hey, it sounds like an emergency."

"Sure does. Take her out of turn. She can't wait."

A guard moved along the seats. "Keep it down, ladies." Boyd Tiller pulled out his filleting knife and poked the tip under Paz' chin. He drew it lightly over her lips to her nose. Her bowels voided. She fainted.

"Holy shit!" The guard leaped, struggled to untangle his feet and put distance between himself and the nightmare.

Another guard, a woman, laughed from a safe distance. "Kinda brings the phrase home to roost, don't it."

Hayhill went aft to take charge. "Get that woman to the lavatory. Damn it. Move! Drag her back there. Find a bucket and plenty of paper towels. Pam. Darcy. You women get her cleaned up."

"Why us? How 'bout ol' Boyd? He caused the problem."

"Do it! Damn it! That's an order."

Madison vacated the lavatory as the guards arrived with Paz. "I'll do it," she said. "Get some water. Lay her out on the floor. Any plastic sheeting?"

When the young woman she would know later as Elaine came out of another lavatory, she pitched in too. "Thanks," said Madison. "I'm either up or down. Bum knee. I'll help her get cleaned off if you bring what I need. Do they have a change of clothes? A pair of pants, for Pete's sake?"

One of the female guards offered a pair of jeans. Madison looked into her face a long moment. "Thanks."

* * *

Later, two male guards pulled a rotation in the women's section and swaggered among the detainees. Madison observed them from the invisibility of her gray hair and slumped posture. Neither wore a uniform. They had military haircuts, but one had dirty fingernails and the other wore scuffed combat boots. The red-haired, ragged-nailed guard had a freckled, regular face, like a kid from a Minnesota dairy farm. Power infected the ruddy complexion of the older man. Tiller wore a boning knife sheathed on his belt. The guards took an interest in a young woman shackled next to her mother.

"Thirteen? Really? You look older, much older," said the man known as Tiller. "You wouldn't lie to us? Not good to lie to representatives of the US government."

The young woman shook her head.

"Man, look at those eyelashes. Like Cleopatra." Tiller ran the back of his hand up and down her cheek.

"Leave her alone. Please, leave her alone." The mother began to hyperventilate.

"No sweat, mama-san. A friendly chat. Don't get all excited." His eyes went overly wide. He wiggled his head implying the mother was silly. "Nothing's happenin'."

Tiller cupped the girl's neck and head when she tried to turn away. His other hand moved from her shacked hand to her shoulder. "Laugh for me."

"Laugh? Why?"

"Please," said the mother. "Please don't." The man put his finger to his lips, then pointed at her before he returned his attention to the girl.

"I want to hear you laugh."

Although he wasn't hurting the girl, Madison saw tension harden his face. He encouraged the girl's nervous laughter, ignored her innocent, unspoken plea.

"Creep." Elaine, Madison's seat mate, leaned and whispered. The engine noise covered their sounds.

"Too many witnesses," said Madison barely moving her lips. "Later. Danger, later."

Hayhill's stern voice blared over the intercom. "Tiller, report forward. On the double."

* * *

Madison pulled into herself, summoning inner strength. Only once before in her life had she been so completely at the mercy of others. She knew what to do.

She invited death into her mind and began a dialogue. Her blank expression portrayed nothing of her internal transformation. She'd had the dialogue years earlier in a car with five other college kids doing ninety plus on the Nimitz Freeway between Berkeley and San Jose. Stuck in the back seat with her blind date, she prayed for the Highway Patrol, but no siren or flashing lights slowed the driver. Panic rose, then control. Control at the price of death. When she gave herself up for dead, her composure returned. She'd learned a lesson she never forgot. Now she banished her fear the same way, consigned herself to death, sighed and closed her eyes.

* * *

On board the military transport plane flying west over the Pacific, Law Hayhill spoke into the intercom again. "Our medics have a series of inoculations for you, ladies and gentlemen. These are necessary for your continued good health at our destination. You'll receive three shots, and may opt for the tetanus/dyptheria. We recommend it if you haven't had a booster in the last ten years. The other shots are mandatory. We will take you by alternating rows. Our people unlock you and direct you to the rear of the aircraft. Your cooperation is appreciated. My assistant will now read the US Army description of our destination."

"Ladies and gentlemen, we are approaching one of the most disaster-prone areas on the planet. Typhoons strike in any month of the year, although between June and November is usual. The southwestern monsoon brings heavy rain May through November. The northeaster monsoon means heavy rains December through February. Therefore, flood-related diseases flourish. Leptospirosis is common. It comes from the urine of infected rats and is potentially fatal.

Cleanliness is essential. Do not sneak any food items into the barracks areas. Do nothing that may attract rats or other vermin.

"In addition to typhoons, floods, earthquakes, tsumanis, storm surges and volcanic eruptions have all occurred in the recent past."

Madison recognized the scare tactics and tuned out.

"Several species of poisonous snakes… aggressive spiders with poisonous bites … giant lizards … a tremendous problem of trash disposal, rats … hostility toward Americans."

Madison tried to find a comfortable position for her head and returned to her internal dialogue. Their captors certainly don't want any argument about the shots.

Hanna Saunders, a twenty-year-old from Baton Rouge, requested the medics skip her. She told them she had a history of allergies. She pleaded, her voice high with worry.

"Nothing to fear, gal. We give thousands of these." The medics jabbed her in both arms and propelled her back to her seat. Sixteen minutes later Saunders' seatmate noticed a problem. In spite of the orders to keep quiet, she called out. "Hey, this woman's in trouble."

The closest guard frowned and jumped to his feet. "Silence. No talking."

"She can't breathe. She's flopping all around."

"Shut up!" But the big guard saw the problem. He yelled for help and unlocked Saunders' shackles. A second guard came, and they manhandled the young woman to the back of the plane. The noise of the plane could not cover the sounds of a medical emergency for the detainees in the closest rows. Sounds from the dimly lit area where the medics worked drifted to Madison five rows forward. She heard disjointed demands, questions.

"Anaphylactic shock."

"No epinephrine? Adrenaline? None? She didn't have an auto-injector on her?"

"Oxygen. Need oxygen! We're losing her!"

Other sounds crackled the atmosphere inside the huge plane, the performance of an emergency tracheotomy, and later, the paddles to resuscitate the heart. After some discussion with the cockpit, the medics wrapped the body in plastic sheeting.

Chapter 15

Los Altos, March 2004

Problems with her ex-husband made Peach edgy. When friends looked at her askance, she wondered what she'd said. A dramatic change in her life would be good.

Peach finished her Red Cross re-certification and requested Olongapo City, Subic Bay in the Philippines, the camps where the Americans detained their own citizens. She made the decision and finalized her plans. Why dally? She knew the Philippine National Red Cross would take her. No one else requested the assignment. She had two offers for her house. The Los Altos real estate market didn't seem to falter in spite of the persistent bad news in the press, around the country and abroad. The offers made her nervous, but she decided to take fifteen thousand over her asking price and be homeless for a while. With the Philippine assignment, she could focus on how she could help Madison and Ev and other innocent citizens. Her cluttered personal life demanded too much energy.

"I know I'm doing the right thing. I know it," she told Kate when they met at Andronico's Market at the Rancho Shopping Center.

Kate called Cynthia and Sue and the soul-searching began. Peach was not surprised that her friends knew her plans when she arrived for Thursday morning tennis. No one walked onto the court or opened a can of balls. For forty minutes the women talked.

"I've sold my house. It's final in three weeks. A Stanford couple. The husband has a journalism fellowship. Doesn't start until next fall, but they wanted the house. He'll be on leave from the *Detroit Free Press*."

"They bought a house here when they plan to return to Detroit?" Cynthia's frown said she couldn't believe it.

"Their plan is to retire here," said Peach. "The husband's parents live in Palo Alto and the wife's in Marin. Only problem is I may need a place to stay for a week or two. The kids aren't too thrilled about mom moving in with them."

"Peach. Stay with us. Jason and I talked about it," said Cynthia.

Sue looked up, caught the lie, but stayed quiet. Cynthia told Peach which room she would have and how she could help with the cooking and the yard and that she could stay as long as she needed. Cynthia continued so long that Sue glanced at the others. They must recognize Cynthia's rehearsal for telling Jason, or was it something else?

Kate spoke but seemed surprised at her own words. "You'll need cash, Peach. We know you're short until escrow closes. I can give you five hundred dollars today and another five hundred later. Will the Red Cross fly you to Manila?"

Sue noticed that the others didn't seem to realize Peach's house sale would generate cash, but even so, her long-term financial situation wasn't great.

"Only if the US agrees to open the camp to us," said Peach. "If I were in Manila it would be easier. It's not far to Olongapo."

"Jim will put in something too," Kate said. "We discussed it last night."

Sue smiled. Also a lie, but Kate did it better.

"We can help too, Peach." Sue said and put aside her psychological observations. "Which is better, cash or medical supplies? They sometimes give the almost expired medicines to good causes for free. I can see about arranging medical supplies through some of the hospital suppliers, if that's a need." Sue looked at Peach expecting to see her on the verge of tears and happy. Peach's determined expression surprised her. Peach looked like she was lecturing students.

"Thanks, Sue. I'll get back to you. I'm sure there's a need for medicine. What I want to say is Maddy and Ev committed no crime. They need us," Peach said. "We can help them. Thank you. Thank you. Thank you from my soul to yours. We are not mere sunshine patriots, but Washington's soldiers at Valley Forge."

The women pulled out their racquets and played their best tennis of the past ten years.

Chapter 16

After several days, or what seemed like several days in the air, the C-130 landed, taxied a while and bumped to a stop. The air inside the big plane became oppressive. The huge hatchway remained closed. Perspiration stung Madison's eyes.

The rear cargo door opened then a small one somewhere forward. It was night. "At last," said a heavily armed, sweating guard.

Fresh, warm humid air circulated. It smelled of flowers and rain. The tropics? Madison kept alert. She hoped to see Ev, but the men deplaned before the women did.

The detainees moved from the plane to trucks after a brief pass through a dilapidated, poorly lit public toilet facility. Unusually wet weather had triggered a ten-year hatch of bugs. Black gnats covered the floors. They filled the air and landed on everyone. They didn't bite, but they stuck to sweaty skin. The detainees brushed them away from their faces and tried not to breathe or swallow them.

Outside, in the wash of a single sodium light affixed to a utility pole, a powerful looking man worked on the engine of a dull green Gamma Goat. Hutch Okakope ignored the gnats. He wore his shorts low, no shirt and thin flip-flops. A bulldog tattoo on his right shoulder was visible when he paused to wipe his greasy hands on a rag and watch the procession. He had the serious frown of concentration, or disgust. It was a tough, don't mess with me look. His head jerked suddenly. He recognized someone, a balding man, taller than the others. Behind the open hood of the light utility vehicle, his voice a hushed whisper, Hutch said, "Ev?"

Druid looked up, didn't see him.

"Ev, don't you recognize me?"

Ev looked, then gave a quick raised chin sign before both men looked away to see if anyone noticed. Hutch Okakope, a Kona native, continued to tap and lean over the engine, but now he studied the new arrivals, not the engine. The Gamma Goat, bigger than a jeep, had magnetic panels with "Across the Board Contractors" logo and lettering. Hutch had moved his family to Luzon three years earlier, but the income from the machine shop wasn't quite what he'd hoped, and the coffee farm was more like a hobby at this stage. The MPs ordered the men into waiting trucks. Hutch scrutinized the women who reappeared from the restrooms more slowly. Oh, my God! Her too. "Maddy." Again, a little louder, "Madison!"

She turned her head, but her face was blank. The first trucks pulled away. Hutch stood up straight, tilted his head, and flashed the hang loose, shaka sign at her, three middle fingers down with the thumb and little finger extended. She tripped and almost fell in her surprise. Silently, she spoke his name. Madison dawdled. She was the second to last of the women loaded into the last truck. Before a guard pulled the heavy canvas flap down and lashed it into place, Madison held up her hand in the same universal Hawaiian greeting. Few people realize the gesture was once a warning among plantation kids on Oahu that the guard on patrol was near.

In spite of seeing Hutch, Madison, Ev and most of the others knew they were not in Hawaii. They'd flown far too long. From her vantagepoint in the back of the truck Madison pulled the canvas back between the grommets and watched for anything she might recognize. She enjoyed the small puffs of outside air even though it came mixed with diesel fumes. She thought she'd heard the sounds of Tagalog among the ground crew when she left the plane. Peeking out while the truck climbed a hill, she caught sight of a large bay, a lighted harbor and sprawling city. Fifty years had passed since she had visited Manila as a child, but she knew. She knew! The sunken ships in the harbor were gone, but something in the shadowy, sequined outline of the land and black water clicked. "We're in Manila," she said aloud.

"Shut up!" said the sweating woman guard across from her.

They drove north through the night on a twisting road that jostled and bumped the detainees. Madison assumed they headed for Subic Bay. She thought of

Subic and tried to remember every detail from her one visit to the base when she was ten. She remembered the pier, the bridge over a river emptying into the bay, the tiny settlement on stilts. Everything would be different. The US Navy no longer operated the base. She'd heard Olongapo was a modern city.

* * *

Lupe Verdad, Hutch's wife's cousin, found Madison cleaning a toilet stall, putrid and slippery with vomit. She braced herself against the stench, filled her bucket with soapy water and moved to help the older woman who looked up with a smile and a nod of appreciation. When they finished, Lupe ventured a conversation.

"How do you survive here?"

"I tell myself stories."

"What stories?"

"Stories that no one has ever told."

"What if they keep you forever? You can't leave?"

"I leave. I escape in fragments, inside my stories."

"Oh? I get it, I guess. I'm Lupe, by the way. Hutch sent me. Got me the job. Said to watch out for you. He knew you in Kona." She looked to Madison for confirmation. The woman seemed wary and guarded her response. "You took him out fishing with you some times."

"Hutch?"

"Yeah." Lupe hosed out the buckets then dumped the rags into the soapy water in an outside wash tub.

"Supposed to have four washing machines, but I don't see 'em."

"Not much of a job, cleaning toilets." Madison braced her lower back with her hands and tried to relieve the ache. She watched the new woman.

Lupe checked that no one was within earshot. "Hutch said Law Hayhill wants the detainees to think there's a spy in your group. At least one, but if there is, he doesn't know who it is. It's not me. I understand you might be suspicious." Madison's look left no doubt.

Lupe said, "My husband's sick, can barely walk. We have three children. I'm a barracks supervisor. The noon to 6 p.m. shift starting today. Someone's coming!"

Lupe wiped her soapy hands on her colorful tie-dyed shirt and directed Madison to the sink. "And, then get the rags you left in the shower area and wash those." One of the Across the Board contractors passed by and ignored them.

Chapter 17

Subic Bay/Olongapo City March 29, 2004

Law Hayhill shielded his eyes in the slanting sunlight of the long dusk. He didn't look happy about Lieutenant Maris Dugame's arrival. A young ensign drove and pulled up short of the contractor. Madison returned from the shower area in time to witness the exchange. The tone more than the words caught her attention.

"Welcome aboard, lieutenant. Leonard Hayhill, with Across the Board Contractors. You want to meet the staff tonight or tomorrow? I recommend tomorrow."

"I'll do a walk through this evening. Introductions, no address."

"Suit yourself, lieutenant. When would you like to begin?"

"Ten minutes. You have the report I want?"

"On your desk."

"Fine. I'll be with you in ten."

* * *

Madison quickly gathered flowers. She held her government-issue towel by its four corners to hold the yellow and deep red-purple plumeria blossoms she picked. When her towel filled, she looked for other flowers, but rejected the single red ginger blossom at the entrance to the lieutenant's Quonset. It would last longer where it was, and Madison didn't have a knife to saw through the stem. She spotted a red hibiscus plant, tall and rangy, loaded with buds. Hibiscus bloom only one day. Picked, they last no more than a few hours, with or without water. There would be plenty in the morning.

After chow, Elaine watched Madison sitting on her bunk, stringing a lei. "Creating a wedge with flowers, right? That your plan?"

"Flowers can't hurt. Worth a try."

"They won't give us any more sewing supplies if they figure this out, you know."

"I never liked to sew anyway."

Early the next morning Madison asked Lupe for a favor. Lupe took the lei and freshly picked hibiscus to Dugame's office. She hung the lei on a towel rack in the bathroom and arranged the red hibiscus, one on the sink, another on the back of the toilet and clustered a group of five on the lieutenant's desk.

* * *

Lieutenant Maris Dugame, Army Psychological Operations, looked through the water droplets filling in the screen of her Quonset office. The contractors used cinder block for the men's facility, but then there were more men. Bile rose in her throat. Sweat dampened her uniform at the armpits and collar of her tropical khakis. She punched her fist into her left hand over and over. She faced Olongapo, but she didn't see the town in the rainy mist of early morning. She didn't see the steep, jungle-covered mountains, the gray bay fused with the gray sky or the molting black hen scratching at the ground under the steps. Dugame looked inward.

Running a women's prison in the Philippines. Great. After all that's coming to light in Getmo and Iraq and Afghanistan, I get a prison administrator assignment. It's over. Definitely over. Hell, I won't be considered for anything on the outside either. So much for being sixth in my class. Whoopee. Prisoner abuse before I even arrive.

The Navy yanked her from her training mission on Guam. Needed her for an important assignment in Olongapo. Her background was perfect, they'd said. The truth was the Navy needed a female officer, fast. The detainees arrived in the Philippines a week and a half before she did. Technically, the Navy was in violation of the Presidential Finding, although Across the Board Contractors plugged in local women to fill the female guard requirement. The Administration slapped the operation together in a hurry. The military scrambled to catch up. The Philippines, who knew? It was so far from the Middle East.

Footsteps approached. A knock and Lt. Dugame's door opened unbidden. A gray-haired man with creased, leathery skin entered. He stood six two and wore rumbled, government-issue fatigue pants and a green Aloha shirt.

"Lt. Dugame? Law Hayhill, retired Major, Special Forces. I'm with Across the Board contractors. We met briefly when you arrived." Law hesitated. "May I sit, Maris?"

Dugame did not turn around. She blinked back fire when Hayhill used her given name, a deliberate putdown from a man she'd met when she assumed command the previous evening. If he expected the laugh and giggle type, he was dead wrong.

"No." Dugame turned. "What kind of sorry, son-of-bitch outfit you running here, Hayhill? You know the rape of an American citizen, a thirteen-year old for Christsake, would land any soldier or sailor in the brig, then sent home to do hard time."

"Yes ma'am. Tiller didn't realize she was an American citizen."

"You sent that bastard home, back to the States, before I got here. Nothing happens to him."

"Now see here. That's not exactly true. I got worked over by Kenny. I don't need a rehash. When this is all over…"

"Can it, Hayhill. You and I need to cooperate, but independent contractors give me a rash. Don't have the professionalism or the discipline of the military. Government rushed it. Should've waited. Putting you guys in charge until the military got here, huge mistake. Huge."

Retired Major Hayhill's face hardened. He set his jaw, clenched his teeth and stood to attention. "Hell, we built this place. Threw it up in little more than forty-eight hours. Damn near. You know as well as anyone, we do the tough jobs, ma'am. The dirty ones Uncle Sam keeps quiet. The country needs people like us. Shorthanded as the military is, we fill the gaps. You need us.

"So Lieutenant, you just go on back to Manila. Pick up supplies or something. Give us another week here. We'll get the information we're after. Authorize a little 'truth' serum. We're this close." He indicated less than an inch with his thumb and index finger.

"I'm not going back to Manila, Major. Number one. Number two, Persons of Interest are not Enemy Combatants. Raping the kid part of your plan?"

"Unfortunate. Wasn't supposed to go down like that. I already told Kenny. You musta just read the report. We isolated a few of the women, the leaders. Used the kid. Used the threat of harm to get them to talk. Figured the rest would cooperate. I shouldn't have had Tiller take her out. Things got outa hand. He got carried away. Doesn't work for us any more. Fired the bastard."

"A felony committed against an American citizen, and he loses his job. That's it? And, did you notice your tactic didn't work? You got no info."

"The mother blabbed. Couldn't shut her up."

"Nothing. You got nothing. She said whatever she thought would help her daughter. Agreed to everything.

Contradicted herself. Begged. None of the others said anything useful."

"We didn't separate out every leader, is all."

The lieutenant walked over and stood behind her desk, her left hand with her Annapolis ring over her mouth, her eyes closed thinking about Hayhill. She shook her head as if to say, What a dodo. Leadership got these women detained in the first place.

She drew in a long, slow breath through her nose.

"We'll get what you need, Lieutenant. All kinds of things we can do. Rearrange the interviews. We got a few aging hippies, lot of the older boomer generation. Make it look like... Well, you know. No time for all the shots before they flew over. Not all these women are going to make it home. Some are sick. They know it. We know it. Fear works. Give it some time."

"Commander Kenny, USN, is in charge of this operation, Hayhill. He placed me in charge of the women's center. I report to Kenny, and you report to me. Is that clear?"

"Yes, Ma'am." But his expression betrayed his thoughts as clearly as if he'd spoken them: Not for long, you spoiled brat. Rumor has it we're going to Singapore.

"You know very well Kenny isn't happy, Hayhill. I'll work with you, as ordered, but I'd as soon shoot you. So, if there's the slightest hint of insubordination, disrespect or failure to carry out an order, I'll hang you. Clear?"

"Yes, sir. Perfectly clear."

"You have two months, two and a half, tops, to finish your construction work. Kenny's terminated your contract as of 15 June."

A black hen wandered through the doorway, looked around, wandered out again.

"And Hayhill."

"Yes, sir?"

"The hen's our mascot. See that she doesn't die. Pass the word. She dies, disappears, your crew goes on half rations."

"You can't do that! Pardon, sir, but you can't do that."

"Subic is Navy territory, Major. Philippine Government, Philippine Navy or US Navy makes no difference. It means your access to the commissary and the supplies. I remind you, President Arroyo is a woman, and Olongapo's mayor, Kate Gordon, is a woman. One other thing, Kenny likes the hen.

"Report back here at 0930. That'll be all."

If Hayhill knew she was exaggerating her authority, he didn't show it.

Dugame sat down and saw the red hibiscus for the first time. She almost swept them to the floor when she saw a scrap of paper under them.

"A tough assignment for all of us. Your detainees"

Lupe passed by the door and looked inside. Dugame saw her and waved her inside. "What do you know about this?"

"They asked me. The women. Flowers for the new boss. They don't much care for the contractors. Many problems. One girl raped. One died on the plane. Bad things."

* * *

Two sailors sat apart in the enlisted mess area and finished their hurried lunch. Dispersing clerk Tia Martinez said, "She's no pushover, Ruben. Should've heard her. Never heard her talk like that. Not on Guam, not ever. She was pissed."

"Where were you? In the Supply Office?"

"Yeah. I wasn't on her radar screen. Didn't matter if I was there or not. She has a right to be sore."

"Amen. What happened at 0930?"

Tia lifted her left shoulder, waved her fork with her right hand. "She moved the meeting to base command. Keeps the locals in the loop. You know, I wonder if she's pushing Hayhill and his group to bail out before they planned. Private company, they can leave whenever. Just quit. But they like the money."

"Or, they know something we don't. Seems like they keep secrets. Only tell us what they think we know anyway."

* * *

In the plywood building that served as the contractors' barracks, a middle-aged man with a Marine haircut sat facing Hayhill.

"She's bluffing. For sure she's lying about the hen, Law. Hasta be."

93

"Yeah, well, see that we feed the damned thing, and don't let a monitor get it. Hen's the least of our worries. Lota stuff hitting the fan stateside."

Chapter 18

Philippine Islands, March 30, 2004

Peach White arrived at Ninoy Aquino International Airport and found her entry expedited. The long flight tired her. Mildly curious, she didn't argue. Her plan was to grab a cab to the Manila Hotel and contact the Philippine Red Cross the next morning.

A handsome Filipino gentleman extended his hand and smiled. He stood a half, maybe a whole, inch taller than she. His eyes met and held hers.

"Roberto Sanchez. I'm with President Arroyo's office, liaison with the Red Cross and other NGO's. I'm very pleased to meet you." He spoke with a comfortable slowness and total focus that disarmed Peach.

"How nice. I didn't expect anyone…"

"I assure you the pleasure is mine."

"Oh, well. It's great." Peach broke eye contact. She made a helpless gesture with right hand. "I wondered about managing three bags."

Roberto Sanchez waited patiently with her for her bags. Peach saw him scan the crowd several

95

times. Airport personnel appeared deferential. When the Chief of Security walked through their baggage area, the men acknowledged each other with slight movements of their heads. Whenever Sanchez looked her way his face was radiant. Tired or not, Peach had some questions.

"Tell me, how do I rate someone from the President's office?" Peach said as they waited.

"My car is right outside," he said. The uniformed driver came forward, bowed his head slightly to Peach, and collected her luggage. They followed him outside and waited while he loaded it in the trunk. "I'm sure you're quite tired," said Sanchez. "Will you have breakfast with me at your hotel at 7:30 or 8 AM? I know you have a meeting at ten."

Peach blinked. *How does he know that? I haven't even called for an appointment yet.* "If you don't tell me what this is about, I'll be in worse shape tomorrow. I'll spend the night trying to figure out what's going on."

"It isn't that dramatic." Sanchez laughed. "I could take care of it tonight, but then I'd miss the chance to have breakfast with a beautiful woman."

"Oh, give me a break."

Sanchez raised an eyebrow. "You know there is a presidential election this June?"

"So I understand."

In the same satin sheet voice he said, "President Arroyo wants no problems with the facility you will be inspecting. The abuses in Iraq must not be repeated here. The US pressure weighs heavily on my country. You call it carrots and sticks."

Peach stiffened, on guard. She dipped her chin and her hands came up, palms out.

"Don't misunderstand, Mrs. White."

"Just Peach White. Husband left after thirty-seven years." Peach couldn't believe she said it so casually.

"I think he is a fool." Roberto Sanchez lowered his eyes and brought them back to her face. "But about why I met your plane, let me say that my government wants you to do your job." His face was serious, watchful. A hank of groomed hair fell across his forehead. His voice came with his same deliberate slowness that gave each word power. "You must do your job, but we need to know immediately if anything is amiss. We have sources, of course, but we require copies of the official Red Cross reports as well. Your government agreed to this. All the same, we want to ensure the people on the ground observe the agreement. Our government has too much at stake for scandal. We know of the death on the plane and rape."

Peach's mouth opened. "What?" She swallowed hard.

"It has not been reported yet, but it will come out this week. Your government wanted time to notify the families. And, we think, to devise an excuse."

"My God! Who died? How? A rape?"

"The death on the plane was due to an allergic reaction, a terrible accident. It was a young woman from Louisiana. The other…We have agreed to give your government an indefinite period to investigate the rape. The alleged guilty party is back in the US, uncharged. You need to document the incident, talk to the victim, to witnesses and to those with knowledge of the crime."

"Not alleged crime?"

"No. We have a copy of the report from the hospital in Olongapo."

Peach's head ached. She rubbed her forehead with her fingertips a moment. She put her hands down and said, "Of course."

They spoke no more until the car pulled up to the Manila Hotel.

"Here we are, an interesting choice. My favorite. This grand old lady was built in 1912 and has been restored many times.

"A friend told me she'd visited it as a child. I could have stayed somewhere more modern or cheaper, but I decided to treat myself for a couple of nights before I go to Olongapo. Foolish, I suppose."

The concierge came forward and greeted them as they stepped from the car. Definitely not the Red Cross treatment Peach remembered. "Why did I go into teaching?" she said.

"Pardon?" the concierge leaned closer.

"Nothing. Everything is very nice."

Sanchez left with a promise of breakfast in the morning. The elegant hotel reflected its Spanish-Philippine heritage. Her room overlooked Manila Bay. Peach, tired and aware she was not doing her best thinking, pulled out her paperwork and scanned her orders. Yes, it was there.

In a single sentence she found the reference to shared reports with the government of the Philippines. A single sentence, that was all. Peach saw another problem, a possible ethical trap. She decided she'd clear it up in the morning.

As she explained to Sanchez over breakfast, she needed to pay her own expenses. She didn't want to offend the government or the hotel or anyone, but it was important for her independence of thought and judgment. Sanchez readily agreed then changed the subject to jai alai.

"Have you ever attended the games?"

"No, I don't really know anything about the sport," said Peach, sipping the last of her coffee. She listened to the cadences of his speech, smooth and flowing even in his excitement for jai alai.

"It's a little like handball. You have a three-walled court with two, four or six players. They use a *cesta* to catch and throw the ball." Sanchez paused when he saw her questioning look.

"I'm a tennis player," she said. "What's a *cesta*? The thing they wear on their wrists?"

"Yes. It's a like a long, curved woven basket." He gestured with his arms. Very thrilling game. Very fast. Much faster than tennis. We sit above and watch all the action."

Peach gave him a negative, wrinkled nose smile, one that said, no thanks. "Perhaps before I return to the US. I haven't recovered from the trip…"

"The energy in the arena infects you. Makes you feel alive."

"There's a tango demonstration in the main ballroom this evening, a group from Argentina. If I'm up to it, that's what I'd really like to see."

"Of course, it's settled. I will made arrangements."

"Okay."

"You like the tango. I do too. Very sexy. No problem for you if I arrange it?"

"The tango's different." Peach laughed. "An exception."

"Ah."

He rode the light rail system with Peach to the Philippine Red Cross headquarters, gave her his card and took his leave. You can take the light rail back or catch a…"

"I'll be fine. Thank you."

"Very good. I'll see you this evening. Argentine tango instead of Philippine jai alai, you're sure?" His eyes sparkled and made her laugh.

* * *

Introductions and briefing sessions took the morning and ran into late afternoon. Peach received her travel packet for the following day. Travel by boat to Olongapo and her hotel accommodation vouchers until the US Navy decided where she could stay at the facility. Her Philippine counterpart said she might want to say in Olongapo City as long as possible rather than getting stuck at the women's detention facility, but Peach made no protest.

She had the impression that the Navy had little notice she was on her way. When she saw the report of the detainee's death on CNN, the weight of her role hit her. I'm standing on a chessboard, she wrote in her diary, but I don't know which piece I am.

* * *

Sanchez and his driver saw Peach off. His gaze level, he asked, "You know a detainee?"

Peach's mouth opened than closed. It took an instant, but he saw it.

"I…I suppose it's possible," she said. "I haven't seen the lists. There might be someone I know."

Sanchez could not stop one corner of his mouth from curving up. "Our relationship with the US Navy is excellent. They will make the lists available to the Red Cross." He held out his hand, "Good luck to you, Peach White." He held her hand in his. "You'll do an excellent job."

* * *

Peach checked into her hotel in Olongapo and congratulated herself on her decision to spend two nights in elegance in Manila. She reported to the US Women's Detention Facility. Lieutenant Maris Dugame intimidated her when they met.

"Glad you here, Oralee. We can use you. This is Chief Petty Officer Flo Boatwick. She has a pretty good medical background, so in emergency medical matters we generally defer to her.

"It's Peach."

"Beg pardon?"

"Please call me Peach White."

The lieutenant continued as if she hadn't heard. "Operationally, I'm CO of this facility. I report to Commander Kenny in Manila. Law Hayhill heads up the contractors, construction, public works, facilities. Law reports to me, but it's hard for him." Dugame glanced up with a hard smile.

"Peach? Warm and fuzzy?" She paused. "No offense, but one's as bad as the other. Okay, I'll start over. Glad you're here, Peach." Maris Dugame grinned.

Peach didn't see Madison in the mess hall at noon, but pushed aside her worry. She returned to her room in town at dusk, happy about the lighter tone her nickname created. Happy until she reviewed Hayhill's report of the death on the plane and the rape of the thirteen year old.

The next day she helped Flo with inoculations and record keeping. In the middle of the medical supply inventory, Dugame came by with the detainee list for the women's facility. She suggested Peach visit the men's facility the next day. Dugame returned to her office, and Flo left Peach to finish the inventory. A familiar voice said, "Don't forget the anti-venom stuff."

"Anti-venom! Snakes? Who said that?" Peach swung around. "Maddy!"

Maddy's finger went to her lips. They hugged. Tears washed their cheeks, but Maddy laughed. "I shouldn't have done that. I know you are irrational about snakes."

"Maddy, it's you. They don't have snakes here, really? I don't do snakes, Maddy."

"I remember. You volunteer for this? For us?"

"Yeah. Dumb, huh? I'd only come to a place with all these bugs and lizards for really good friends. Didn't know about the snakes."

The medical corpsman came through the door. Peach turned to the cabinets and spoke like a professional liar. "Oh, Flo, where do we keep the anti-diarrheal medicine?"

* * *

Lt. Dugame made sure they were alone. "I'll make you a deal, Peach. If anyone guesses who it is you knew before you came here, you're gone. Understand? You are here to help each and every detainee without any hint of favoritism. Clear?"

"Yes. Absolutely."

"Just because my career is shot to hell, doesn't mean I won't do the best, most professional job I can."

"I feel the same way. I won't let you down."

Neither woman mentioned the Druids. Peach didn't know if Dugame really knew something or merely suspected it. Dugame did her homework. She had uncovered the Los Altos connection, but Peach didn't know this until the end.

In bed that night, Peach wrote, Maybe I'm the knight, jumping around the board in every direction. Or just a pawn, moving forward one or two paces at a time.

Chapter 19

Los Angeles, April 4, 2004

In Southern California, about sixty miles northeast of Los Angeles, Lena Hunterson's miniature Schnauzer awoke her at 4:37 AM. He chased around the bedroom, leaped on her bed and off again before hiding under it.

* * *

"Excuse me, Cynthia." Peach drew stares from the other women around the table in the Forest Vista Tennis Club. Kate frowned and put her index finger up to her lips. Peach recoiled. "I…I just wondered who Lena Hunterson was. That's all. I didn't mean to interrupt the story."

"Jason's great-aunt."

* * *

When Lena eventually pulled her little dog out, he was quivering and whining. Nothing she did seemed to comfort him. The local newscaster on her morning television station at 5 AM reported the Humane Society had an unusual number of calls for lost pets the previous day. The newscaster's own cat was missing. A Cal Tech scientist proposed the recent swarm of earthquakes along the San Andreas Fault near San Diego might be affecting the animals.

Lena took her nervous pet for a three-mile walk, all the way to the park. It didn't help. When she headed back to her condo, the dog refused to walk. She picked up the quivering little thing and wondered aloud if he was having a stroke. At 7:03 AM the quake hit. Lena didn't remember being tossed to the ground, but she hit hard. She lay still, waited for stars to clear from her head and tried to understand. She still had her little dog snugly in her arms. The blaring of car alarms, burglar alarms, then sirens filled the dusty air. She didn't understand why it was so dusty. When she stood up at last, she worked to orient herself. Her Schnauzer struggled and tried to bite her. She wrapped his leash twice around her hand and put him down. He whined and trembled. It was several moments before Lena realized her building lay in rubble.

Four hundred miles to the north, Randy Salazar had started his day early as he sat on a hard metal chair pulled up to a gray metal table in a cavernous sub-basement in the San Francisco Police archives. In the previous two days he'd gone through thousands of photos of the April 1996 march. From clues in the account Madison wrote of the day, he narrowed his search to a group of about eighty photos. He had the Asian Law Students banner in three pictures and began from there when the news filtered down that a Magnitude 7.2 quake had struck Los Angeles.

An attendant said, "Better finish up, pal. We've gone on alert. You got five minutes to clear out. That's all. Think they might have up to twenty-five thousand casualties."

The attendant left, and Randy scribbled a note. He placed the note in the manila folder, returned the folder to the box and gathered up the photos spread on the table before him. He slipped the photos into his personal, leather folder then thought better of it and returned them to the file. He knew the quake would be the only story for a long while. All the ink goes to the disaster.

The cop who observed the whole thing let it slide. The guy put the photos back. Besides, arresting reporters was always messy.

Chapter 20

San Francisco and Washington, DC

The Ninth Circuit Court of Appeals had the detainees' case, Gleason, Stockmeir, et. al. v. the United States, on its docket but delayed to await the Supreme Court's ruling on the Guantanamo Bay cases expected in July. Gleason, Stockmeir, et. al. included Madison and Evert Druid and the others detained under the findings signed by the President in February. The Federal District Court in San Francisco granted Habeas Corpus, but the Federal Government appealed. While they were citizens, the applicants were not in the United States. They were held in Philippines, on Philippine soil, under an agreement with the Philippine government. Hearings would be conducted with "all deliberate speed, just as soon as possible."

The Administration denied the families visiting rights, denied all visitors, except the Red Cross. Both a Philippine and a US Red Cross representative were onsite. If the Administration was surprised, it appeared not to show it. When Commander Kenny took command in early March, he had launched his own preemptive strike. He commented to a CNN reporter that the US Navy would abide by the letter of the agreement with the Philippines.

"Yes, including the provision for Red Cross monitoring. Of course. The Philippines and the US each have a monitor on site as we speak." In an aside, he was heard to say, "I run a clean ship. Damn it."

The admiral chewed him out for talking to the press, but politically the Administration could not pull back from the Red Cross agreement. The Administration had more pressing matters to attend.

* * *

The President's Press Secretary dribbled information at the afternoon's news conference as if it were an afterthought. When asked about individuals, he checked his notes, then said, "I remind you that these detainees are dangerous individuals, radicals. They're card-carrying members of fringe organizations. Most belong to ten or more of these groups. Groups that work against the President's policies, undermine our troops and hamper the War on Terror."

Baited by a reporter he rarely called upon, the Press Secretary remembered too late why he didn't call on him. The reporter bugged him. Words came out of Press Secretary's mouth without thought.

"Okay, I'll give you an example. I'll just pick one." He pulled a sheet from his folder. Other sheets fell to the floor. "Help me with these." An aide gathered the papers and handed them to the Press Secretary.

"Here. This is one Madison Druid from Northern California, picked up at the Oakland Airport." What the hell, California went to the Democrats last time around, probably will again.

"She's typical of the others. Here's a sample of her memberships: ACLU, NOW, Religious Coalition for Abortion Rights, Planned Parenthood, Amnesty International, Americans for Separation of Church and State, Moveon.org, contributions to, couple gun control outfits, let's see, one, two, … six, ten women's organizations all over, Africa, Asia, India, Latin America. What a bleeding heart! Registered for the UN conference on world government to be held in San Francisco this June. She's known for telling her government students they could advocate the overthrow of the government so long as they didn't set a time and place. Can you imagine?"

"So this person is a teacher?" The reporter's question struck through the stunned press corps.

"It's a woman. Retired teacher."

"When did she retire?"

"Looks like six or seven years ago."

"Before 9/11, then?"

"It doesn't matter. She's disloyal. A dangerous radical. We have our soldiers' lives at stake here. We need unity. We need to pull together. She's the kind of person who threatens the morals and values of our great country and the lives of our brave young men and women." The Press Secretary's face reddened. His voice rose. "She's a '60's Berkeley grad, for God— For goodness sakes! Here's a police photo of her marching in San Francisco. He waved a dark glossy in the air. At last he noticed the silent press corps, staring at him. "I'll have more information for you later." He shoved his papers together with both hands and fled down the corridor with his aide in tow.

The reporter who triggered the outburst gently elbowed a colleague on his right. "A dangerous radical?"

The colleague wore a gold class ring with a deep blue sapphire and the words University of California, Let There Be Light. He raised his eyebrows and sighed, but said nothing.

Chapter 21

May 2004

Hutch tinkered with the new industrial-sized washer that had fallen from a truck onto the concrete and refused to work. Madison saw him and picked up one of the baskets of sheets Elaine collected and hauled it to the open-air laundry. Elaine didn't mind. She flared one elbow and nodded in a go-ahead signal to Madison. Hutch worked on the washer motor with a wrench and gentle words.

"So good to see you, Hutch. You're someone from the time I had a life."

Hutch looked up then around the area. "Aloha, Maddy. Ev's at the men's camp. Said to tell you he's okay. He's good." Hutch shook his head. "All this is crazy. Two of the nicest people I know. You're not helping enemy terrorists. Anyone knows that. It's true for all the people here, I'm positive."

"Haven't seen you in Kona for a while. How'd you get here?"

"We've been here in Olongapo three years. Wife's family's here. Have some land. Grow a little coffee. My partner and I started a machine shop in town."

"Three years. That long?" She looked around and kicked at the cement paving where muddy water undulated toward a drain on the other side. "Don't get caught talking to me."

"Yeah, three years." Hutch turned his toughest frown on the compound, then relaxed. "Got hired 'cuz I can fix most anything. And, for my tough looks. Hayhill's taller, but I'm scarier."

Madison smiled. It felt good. She remembered when she used to smile.

Hutch's mouth suddenly hardened and twisted as he spoke. "And plants along that fence." He swung around and pointed along the perimeter fence. His teeth showed. Madison heard boots on gravel. She slumped and nodded.

"Hutch! What's going on?" Hayhill's voice. Madison turned and moved back. Hutch turned and stepped forward.

"Place needs some sprucing-up, boss. I think these women should put in some plants. Make the place look better and hold the soil." He waved his hand in the direction of the muddy runoff.

"We're not buying plants for a detention center. We didn't scrape everything off. We left a couple trees and bushes. What're you thinking?"

"Didn't say buy, sir. I make cuttings. No cost. The labor's free, too." He indicated Madison and Elaine with his thumb. The women busied themselves loading the washers. "The men work on projects for the city. Women need da kine, you know. Plenty work on my coffee farm. The women could do it. Landscape this place and work on the coffee. Keep 'em busy and out of trouble."

Hayhill rubbed his jaw. "Umm. I'll run it by the lieutenant. You might be right about that, Hutch. Carry on."

Maybe he thought the idea would ease his strained relationship with Dugame.

Chapter 22

May 2004

All seventy-two detainees in the women's facility volunteered to help with the landscaping and coffee cultivation. Lt. Dugame discussed the idea with Hutch and worked out the logistics.

"We'll have more success if he can take credit for the idea," said Dugame. "Tell him I like his idea, and if we pull off the landscaping before Kenny's next inspection, I'd view his effort as very commendable. Use that word, commend-able."

Hutch smiled in spite of himself. He brought up his hand and tried to wipe the smile away. He left Dugame's office and went to find Hayhill.

When he heard about all the volunteers, the contractor scratched his chin and said, "Hmm." He turned to Hutch. "How many do you need?"

Hutch thought and then said, "Let me take ten or fifteen, train them so they can train the rest, and we'll have things done pretty quick."

"You don't think any of 'em will try to run off?"

"Nah. Where to? They got nowhere to go, boss. Most women don't like big lizards, snakes, da kine, you know." He laughed.

"Well, if any do take off, you're responsible, Hutch. You, personally. Got it?"

"Yes, sir, boss. No problem."

"I'll send the guard detail with you when you take 'em up to your place."

"Okay, boss. That's a good idea."

"And, Hutch. No matter what, don't let any guard go off alone with a detainee."

"No, boss."

* * *

When Hayhill visited the first day's training, he learned more than he wanted about coffee. Hutch was in his element. His voice took on authority. Gone was his Hawaiian casual.

"First of all, I want to thank the Kona Growers' Association, Jim Keenan and Dennis Mock Chew, friends and coffee growers on the Big Island. They taught me what I know about coffee." Hutch raised both hands in a gesture of thanks and began his orientation session.

"This red piece of equipment is the pulper. Freshly picked cherry must be processed within two to four hours, or it spoils. The cherry is poured into this chute on top." He ran his hands gently over the equipment. "The drum inside has sharp protrusions, like a grater, that score the skins, then metal bars squeeze the seed out into a chute to the collection tray. The pulp and other stuff falls down here." He pointed.

"This one of your machines, Hutch? You make it?" Hayhill announced his presence.

"No, sir. This machine came from Columbia. I made some of these and adapted some of the rest." Hutch waited a second, but Hayhill didn't ask anything else.

"After the pulper we have a seed covered with sticky, slimy mucilage. This stuff, mucilage, does not wash off. The seeds have to ferment for sixteen to twenty-four hours before the nasty gunk can be washed away. These are the fermentation tanks." He held up two large plastic buckets from a group of ten. Some of the women smiled and nodded.

"After washing, the bean has to dry until the hard outer shell can be removed without crushing the bean. That's what we do with these high-tech, solar trays here." He held up one of his homemade drying trays. More women smiled. They started to understand the tough guy's a sense of humor.

"Once the bean is dried, we refer to it as parchment. I can store parchment for several months some times. This green, meat-grinder type machine does the hulling. I load the parchment into the hopper. A screw forces it into a chamber where the parchment is rubbed against itself under enough pressure just until the shell breaks and frees the green coffee bean. It takes several trips through the huller to get the beans. This machine came from England.

"Now we have a whole bunch of chaff and some green beans. Winnowing is the next step. I place the mix into the winnowing chamber and force air through it. The winnowing chamber is a multipurpose unit." Hutch held up a tall wastebasket. "This unit would be washed and dried." Next, he held up his air source, a shop vacuum. Open laughter broke out. "Chaff flies into the air, and the heavier bean remains in the winnowing chamber, most of the time.

"We almost have what's called a coffee bean. The bean has a very fine white, onion skin-like substance on it that must be polished away. At this point we remove any broken beans. Next, we have my own invention.

"I've fitted the polisher separator, this white pipe with shop vac attached, with a special filter. Hutch held up a colander. Now I let the coffee freely tumble in the polishing chamber. I also invented the mobile and compact equipment mobilizer, made from a couple old wheels I had lying around." He pulled what looked like a cage on a green wagon in front of the gathering."

Hayhill left before the end of Hutch's talk, but Hutch's enthusiasm didn't change.

"The beans need grading and sorting. We have to remove any that are incompletely processed or that are inferior. At last we have green coffee beans, ready for roasting, brewing and drinking."

Hayhill heard the women's applause. "Must be hard-up for entertainment," he mumbled.

* * *

For two weeks, the scheme worked on all levels. Hutch found make-work projects for the women when the processing duties fell short. They went through the motions, but there was not enough cherry at any one time to make the coffee processing worthwhile. Soon, the detainees worked in two large groups instead of several smaller ones. Some battled the weeds encroaching on Hutch's coffee trees, others made cuttings from a variety of shrubs and trees and planted them in the compound and rigged a drip irrigation system. Hayhill questioned the need for irrigation with all the rain, but let it go. He decided it was better to keep the women busy. The camp ran smoother.

That morning he'd witnessed a guard at the entrance to the women's facility even call out a cheery, "Hey, where y'all goin' this morning?"

"Prayer meeting," came one answer.

"Sewing circle."

"Garden Club."

"Yeah, right." The guard waved them through.

* * *

Up slope, or mauka, as Hutch called it, Madison and the young social worker named Elaine decided to take more cuttings. They had plumeria and moved toward another flowering tree neither could identify. They moved closer through dense growth. Elaine tripped. She saw a flicker of movement as she fell. Instinctively she grabbed.

"Uh!"

"Elaine? You okay?"

"Stay back! Madison, stay back! It came right at me!"

A small, green snake, no larger than a person's finger in diameter, lashed around Elaine's left wrist. By chance she'd grabbed the reptile by its head. Two eyes glared and its tongue lashed between Elaine's thumb and forefinger.

Madison dumped the contents from the dirty canvas cuttings sack she carried. "Here! I'll hold this open. Probably poisonous, Elaine. Shake it real hard and drop it in here."

"No! I'm afraid to let go! What if it stays on me? It's wrapped around my hand!"

"You could toss it, and we could run, but they're fast. We might fall."

"Open the sack!" The snake struggled violently. Elaine held it just inside the bag, gave it a shake and dropped it. Madison twisted the top shut and held it out from her body.

One of the guards saw the two detainees wander off and came after them. "What'd you find? Let's see."

"Snake!" Elaine said.

"Oh, sure. Like I'm going to believe that. Let me see."

Madison clutched the throat of the sack. Unable to find her voice, she jerked her head in refusal. She stood still with no expression, her fists squeezed round the canvas sack.

"Hand it over." The guard grabbed the sack and plunged his hand inside. Time stopped. A bellow struggled free of his throat. "Snake bit me!" The snake dangled from his wrist and fingers, dropped to the ground and disappeared.

Madison found her voice. "Sit down! Stay calm! Someone run for help."

"Snake bite!" Elaine screamed to other detainees. "Get help!"

"Make a tourniquet," someone yelled back.

"Aaargh!" The guard dropped his gun, started down the hill, tripped and crashed to the ground. A rock opened a savage cut on his cheekbone. He half-rose, his face contorted. "The medic — Need the medic."

Madison kicked his automatic rifle away and sat on him. "Listen to me. Remember your training. No panic! The faster your heart beats, the faster the poison moves." She paused. "You okay now?"

"Yeah. If you get off me. Yeah."

"Can't see the fangs, but they're so tiny, I bet they're still in you." Madison stood up. "Anything we can use as a tourniquet?"

"How 'bout his belt?" Elaine said.

Madison looked at the man's middle where his belt embedded itself in a fold of flesh. A black line began coursing up a vein in the man's wrist. She whipped off her shirt and unhooked her grimy bra. "A stick! A strong stick!"

The swelling began, but Madison saw no puncture wounds. She tied her bra around his arm, just below the elbow. "Where's the stick?"

"We're looking!"

"Here. Will this work?"

"I'll use it until we find a stronger one."

"Here! Here! I got one."

"Perfect." Madison snatched the sturdy green branch, shoved it into her impromptu tourniquet, and twisted.

"Ow! You're cutting off the circulation."

"Want the poison throughout your whole body?"

"I know. I know."

"Hope you appreciate this is my only bra."

"I'm appreciating."

Madison looked up. The guard smirked sheepishly.

"You toad. I'm old enough to be your mother. Maybe your grandmother." She swung her head toward Elaine. "Need a little coverage here."

Elaine picked up Madison's shirt, turned it right side out and pulled it over Maddy's head. She gave guard a mean frown.

The guard seemed defensive. "Hey, I'm alive. A guy tends to notice."

"I want you to take some deep breaths. Relax," said Madison. "Don't think about the snakebite."

"I ain't, mama. Believe me, I ain't."

"They're coming!" Elaine pointed. "Flo and three guys. Got a stretcher with 'em."

In minutes the scene became more chaotic. "Back off, you women. Back off! Meese! Where's your weapon? Where the hell's your weapon?"

"Musta dropped it. It's here somewhere. The Navy MP swore a string of expletives and turned red in the face. "They could've killed us!"

"No, they wouldn't neither! Now, you goin'a let Flo take a look at my hand and stop swearing in front of the ladies? I been snakebit."

Flo said, "I've read about this. We need to get the fangs out." The way she said it did not inspire confidence. "The book said they're real hard to see."

The women watched in silence. The men recovered the weapon and strapped Meese to the stretcher. Flo asked if they still had the snake. "Be nice to ID it."

As Flo and the men hustled off, Meese called out, "See ya later, mama. Thanks."

Chapter 23

June 2004

Ode to a toothbrush — Lupe gave me a toothbrush today, a new toothbrush still in its original package, and Peach gave me a ballpoint pen! What sweet joy these simple things give me. I cried. My stub of a pencil was finished. I hid it in my mattress, and couldn't retrieve it. A toothbrush and a pen, my heart is glad. If Hayhill used kindness, he might be more successful in his interrogations.

No, I take that back. He assumes we're unpatriotic. No one I've met is unpatriotic. We all support our nation's highest ideals and despair at the path of tyrants our President has chosen. If I sound a bit extreme, consider what they have done to us and remember: Tyranny always arrives wrapped in the colors of patriotism, tied with the bloody ribbon of nationalism.

But I've learned some things, too. I understand friendship better. A friend glimpses my soul and accepts me. A friend does not have to be near in an emergency, although Peach is a great comfort. A friend acknowledges a positive connection in time, an instant or a lifetime. The connection can be large as love or small as a smile, a look, a shared understanding. In matters of friendship I have great wealth, and I draw strength. A fellow teacher always greeted me with "Hello, friend" the most honorable of titles. I hope I've been worthy.

Peach is here. She came for my sake. She came for Ev, too, but especially for me. She helps so many of us. Thank you Los Altos friends. I know what risks you take and what you sacrificed for me. And, I understand more fully than you do what you may yet sacrifice. Please be as careful as you can without abandoning your ideals. I ask that you no longer worry for me. My return is in doubt. Life is sweet, but mine is ending. Comfort Ev, if he makes it home. He is the great love of my life. Ev and I are lucky beyond measure. Comfort our sons and their families with your love. Remind them that they are the source of our greatest joys. Tell them we want them to live in happiness, not to linger on sadness.

Chapter 24

Olongapo

It had not taken long for those who ran the detention center to realize they guarded a sad group of harmless souls. The interrogations went nowhere. Hayhill reported that most detainees simply stopped talking. Those who talked said nothing valuable. The men found the inside listening devices immediately and destroyed them.

"No point putting 'em back. Some electronics experts in the group. And the women—" Hayhill's left hand flew up, grazing his head. "They didn't find the devices. Or, maybe they did and deliberately left them in place. They suspect we're listening. They do things just to irritate us."

"Like what?" Dugame pursed her lips.

"Like those transcripts on your desk. Among themselves some women talk. Some don't.

Hayhill left. Dugame sat down and pulled out the printed transcripts in front of her. On her laptop, she checked out the supposed names and backgrounds of the speakers when the transcripts identified them.

Two young French literature majors, a retired teacher, two unidentified. French Lit? How was French Lit subversive? Whatever. The women had discussed who could remember quotes from Albert Camus that applied to the current situation. Long pauses noted in parentheses punctuated the record.

* * *

Yvette, depressed and filthy, came to life in the cloud-flickered moonlight that flashed through the screens. Her high, ethereal voice riveted everyone's attention. "I have realized that we all have plague, and I have lost my peace."

Madison's fingers tapped her lips and her eyes closed. Katrina, snatched from grad school at Duke, quoted, "All I maintain is that on this earth there are pestilences and there are victims, and it's up to us, so far as possible, not to join forces with the pestilences."

Voices out of the darkness said, "Amen. Amen."

As a couple others supplied quotes, Madison remembered another of the doctor's quotes in *The Plague* and spoke his words. "I only know that one must do what one can to cease being plague-stricken, and that's the only way in which we can hope for peace or, failing that, a decent death."

Someone sobbed. Yvette spoke again, "…love is never strong enough to find the words befitting it." Tears washed paths through the grime on her cheeks.

Madison went to her and put an arm around her shoulders. "I don't agree with that one. Words fail, love doesn't. If we cannot find the right words, or we fail to say the words, it doesn't lessen love."

* * *

"Think I'm goin'a throw up," said the transcriber to his doodles on his yellow legal pad.

* * *

"Isn't that the guy who got bitten by the snake?" Elaine spoke out of the side of her mouth as she and Madison trudged to the laundry area with bundles of sheets. They washed linens every two, or sometimes three weeks, depending on the detergent supply.

"Yeah. His name is Meese. He's coming over."

The contractor glanced around as he approached the women. "Hey, Mama. Wanta thank you for saving my life. Doc in town said I'da died in another few minutes. The fangs were too tiny to see. He put something on the bite that dyed them so he could get them out. He took out seven of the damn things."

Madison gave him a quick nod, a tiny smile and studied him. There was something else. He didn't need to thank her. He looked around again.

"Anything you need? No guarantees, but I'll do my best." Meese made a pretense of poking through the sheets. He watched them load the washers. They didn't stand face to face or look at each other while they talked.

"You'll get in trouble, Maddy," said Elaine. "Either that or this is some kind of a trick."

"Paper," said Madison.

"What?" Meese either didn't hear or didn't understand.

"Paper," Madison said. "For writing."

"That's it? Paper? No medicine? Food?"

"They'll nail you for any of that stuff. Paper's pretty innocent. If you're caught."

"Okay. Sure. That's an easy one. You have more laundry to gather up?"

"Yes, couple more loads," said Elaine.

"Take an extra five, ten minutes inside when you go back for the next load. Don't come out until you see me back here."

On their way back for the rest of the dirty sheets, Elaine said, "Paper? Paper, Maddy?" She gave Madison a shove. "Why not chocolate?"

Maddy and Elaine followed the plan, but they couldn't see the whole laundry area from their barracks. The bell for the noon meal would ring soon. They couldn't wait any longer. Meese was gone, nowhere around.

"Must have been called away," said Maddy. They headed down the row to the last two washers. She opened the first machine and froze. Elaine leaned over and looked. A ream of ink jet paper stood on end inside the washer.

"A ream! That's seven sheets apiece!" Madison clutched her mouth. The bell sounded for chow, and a different contractor headed toward them.

Meese appeared from behind the lavatory area. "I got it, Snyder. Those two have been lollygaging all morning."

* * *

Not everyone thrilled to the prospect of seven sheets of paper. Several women battled deep depression, some were physically ill. Writing provided a therapy of sorts, even though it was hidden. Pencils and pens disappeared from offices. Many women wrote diary notes. Yvette and Tami Sato, a school board member and peace activist from Bolinas, California, folded beautiful origami cranes, a symbol of hope that helped lift spirits however briefly.

Chapter 25

June 2004

"No way! I ain't goin' in there! Already told you. Place stinks to high heaven. So do you. Get away from me. Stand over there. There's nothing I can do."

The twenty-four year old Navy Chief Petty Officer Flo Boatwick waved off the middle-aged detainee who demanded her help. Flo had helped subdue a crazy woman in the bathroom area. The sweating medic had a bruised, swollen left eye, a gash across her nose and another on her knee. Her uniform shirt was ripped and bloody. She looked like the war causality she was. Legs splayed in front of her in the dirt, she leaned against the outside wall of the laundry and pressed a cold can of Mountain Dew to her face.

"She could die. Diarrhea and vomiting. Since 'bout nine last night. She's worse. Slipping in and out of consciousness. We have to get her to the hospital."

"I know. I know. Told Col. Hayhill hours ago. Before the nut case. Dugame and the ensign are in

Manila meeting with Kenny. They're due back. Hayhill said wait for them. Shouldn't have waited."

"You could do more than wait now."

"Yeah, you're right." Flo sighed. "Bring her out. Over there in the shade. I'll see what I can do."

Four of the detainees who'd sat with her all night carried the ill woman outside on her narrow metal bed. The mattress was putrid.

"Oh, God. We better get fluids into her. Lupe! IV's. Saline. On the double!

* * *

"What's her name? Any one find out yet?" Madison stood as quickly as she could with her bad knee. She dropped the trowel and seedling in the hole she'd dug. "It's not Nancy? The one we were up with last night?"

"No. I don't know what her name is. Bunk's the far end of the barracks, fourth from the door. Real quiet. Didn't talk to anyone. She's crackin' up. Broke one of the stall doors half off the hinges."

"Okay. I'm Madison. What's your name?"

"Hillary. Elaine sent me. Said to get you and the long-haired woman. The skinny one, Yvette."

"Hillary?"

"Yeah, one of two Hillarys so far. Think they arrested us because they don't like the name?"

The women tripped and slipped as they hurried down the path back to their compound. Yvette dashed ahead. When they reached the camp the MP waved them through.

A scream, disemboweled with rage and hysteria, greeted them when they entered the shower area. Smeared blood and a broken hypodermic needle, its contents a dark blot on the concrete, littered the floor. The scene of a furious battle unfolded down the row of toilet stalls, one with its door ripped partly off its hinges. Three torn, mismatched flip-flops lay scattered amid shreds of cloth. The smell of disinfectant and sewage permeated the area. Moisture beaded and rolled down the blue-gray paint on the cinderblock walls. Mold colonized the tiny ridges in the cement floors. Bloody traces of scalp and long strands of blond hair stuck to a sharp corner. The wounded woman started to raise her head. Four of the five other detainees stood ready to pounce.

The woman shook. Her arms went rigid. Blank eyes rolled back as she collapsed on the cement floor. Red welts stood out on her face. Someone had tried slapping her out of it. Five bleeding and bruised women leaned against the walls, one with an obvious broken arm. The woman on the floor lay still. Deathly quiet. Someone quickly wound a leather belt around her feet and secured it to a partition post. Madison rushed in and grabbed a roll of paper towels to tuck under the woman's head.

Her name was Logan West, but she was dead before they learned it. She'd snapped and cracked her skull. It was not a case of prisoner abuse, per se. The second death, Nancy, was not as clear-cut. The medical corpsman was too late with the IV.

* * *

On the return from Manila, Commander Kenny drove the military gamma goat. Dugame rode shotgun. The ensign bounced in the back. Kenny discussed Hayhill and the contractors as they approached the women's detention facility.

"He made mistakes, certainly, but the man doesn't condone abuse of the detainees. He's tried to keep his guys under control."

Dugame listened with an occasional non-committal sound or phrase. Her cell phone rang. She pressed the phone to her ear and covered her other ear. Suddenly she yelled at Hayhill. "She died! Another one?"

Kenny swerved, then over-steered to compensate.

Dugame said, "After the one we lost on the plane, you're going down, Hayhill. You better have a damned good explanation!"

On the other end of the line, Hayhill spoke with controlled calm, "We got a second serious problem. Another critical."

"Two? Someone else in trouble?"

"Severe dehydration. Flo says we're too late. One of the women just came to tell me. I'm heading there as we speak."

"What do you mean the medic can't save her? Get her into town! To the hospital."

"Medic says she can't keep fluids in her. It's nasty, lieutenant. . . Hang on. Flo's waving at me."

"Ah, sorry, lieutenant. Flo says that one didn't make it either."

The jeep lurched to a stop by the barracks. Dugame surveyed the scene, cell phone still pressed to her ear. Kenny gripped Dugame's left arm. "Get to the bottom of this, Maris. Two more dead." He looked at the ground. "Find out when the sick call went in. How soon the corpsman reported trouble. What actions were taken. I want to know if anything else could have been done or should be done. No press. Any press people show up, refer 'em to me in Manila."

They approached the disheveled cluster of women by the body on the bed. They stopped short, on the edge of the stench. "Tell me what you need," said Kenny without preamble. No one spoke, so Madison answered. "We need more soap, disinfectant, a plunger, to unstop the toilet, a couple hoses."

Flo found her voice. "Hydrating fluids, IV's, cleaning supplies, sir. Buckets, clean rags. The inside's pretty bad. Especially the toilet and shower area. Couple more women are sick, but none like this. Yet."

"I'll see that you get it," said Kenny.

In Dugame's office Kenny said, "The second detainee, the one dead of a cracked skull, how likely is that? Sure no one took her head and smashed it deliberately?"

"I'll find out what happened, sir. My best guess is what they said, an accident, sir." Lieutenant Dugame held his gaze. She didn't waiver. "I know these women, sir."

"The admiral may or may not require a full-blown inquiry. I can't say. My guess is a postponement, especially if you're right that it was an accident." Get on the horn, to the men's facility, Dugame. Let me talk to Lt. Johnson. Where's a pen?

"Requisition some pens, Maris. There's nothing to write with."

* * *

Ev and two others volunteered to gather what supplies they could and bring them over. They knew it was an emergency. They didn't know two people had died. Hutch drove, Kenny's orders.

In Dugame's office Kenny was on the phone again. "This is Commander Kenny. Put me through to Kate Gordon, the mayor." He turned to Dugame and said, "She can help us out, negotiate with the hospital for what we need." The commander waited, phone to his ear, and watched the compound through the screened window.

Ev recoiled when he saw Madison. He gasped. Tears welled in his eyes. He started for her, but Hutch stopped him.

"Help me with these. Ev, someone might be watching."

Ev ignored him and kept going until he stood before Madison with his hands out in helplessness, fear and love. She had cuts, bruises on her arms and legs. An open sore on her lower lip oozed.

She tried to smile. "I'm okay." She rallied and added, "Nothing a shower and some time in the hot tub won't fix. It's so good to see you."

Ev's head bowed to one side and came back with a nod and a longing in his eyes that Madison knew she would take with her into eternity. He enfolded her in his arms.

Kenny watched from Dugame's office and said, "Those two know each other."

"Yes, sir. Married forty years."

Kenny sighed and shook his head. "Sad. Call me soon as you have your report."

"Aye, aye, sir. You want to talk to Flo Boatwick now?"

"Like to, but gotta get back to Manila tonight. The whole situation here, a fine kettle of fish. What do you think, Maris? Food poisoning?"

"Could be, but it might be anything."

"Ah, Maris."

"Sir?"

"There's no big rush to get those folks back to their compound. Give them some time to talk." He made a quick nod in the direction of the couple embracing outside."

"Aye, aye, sir."

Chapter 26

Breaking News in the US, May and June 2004

At 3:46 AM, with no moon, rancher Harmon Leech pushed the speed limit faster than he should have for his heavy Dodge pickup. Highway 93, out of Arco, Idaho, takes hard 90-degree turns and presents a challenge in daylight. Leech had his music loud when his steering went out. The truck bounced at sixty-five miles an hour. Leech battled what he assumed was the worse flat tire of his life. The truck did not respond to his foot stomping on the breaks. His truck left the pavement, slammed into a ditch and rolled. He felt no pain. Nothing. His last thought, It isn't the truck. Earthquake!

The cold front due over southern Idaho picked up speed. The latest forecast called for high, westerly winds throughout the region for several days. The sparse population in the area limited loss of life to one dead, Leech, and five injured, all in one family, when their roof collapsed. The proximity to the Army's atomic test grounds caused a different problem.

Memories of the massive sheep kill in northern Utah ignited a firestorm among the environmentalists and other people living downwind. Confusion over the Army Medical Institute Infections Research facility at Dugway/Tooele and other military lands in the area stirred old fears. The Administration took notice.

"Who are these nuts? You'd think the quake hit Yucca Mountain or Hanford or Savannah River the way they're yapping. How'd we miss these people?" Department of Homeland Security Secretary Peaks steamed. His cheeks puffed out. His neck reddened. "I've got a meeting with the President and the Secretary of Defense. What am I going to tell them?"

"We could round up the protestors, but I don't advise it, sir," said Undersecretary Mitchell. "Stay calm. With all the casualties coming out of Los Angeles, and now the fires, the Idaho flare-up will be off the front pages by tomorrow. Concentrate on the outpouring of aid, the people coming together to assist Los Angeles."

"Thought the aftershocks spooked everyone. Anyway, we don't want people pouring in."

"True, but communities throughout the US are gathering supplies, clothing, food. The Smokejumpers, other professional firefighters from all over rushing to southern California. That's the story. The media is doing its job for once. Idaho's nothing. One guy drove his truck off the road. Sit tight."

"Okay. Yeah. We fly the President over the devastated area in California tomorrow morning. Maybe the First Lady visits a food distribution station and three of the tent cities. You're right. L.A.'s the story."

But the disasters continued.

* * *

Venessa Almond, Secretary of Agriculture, doggedly resisted public pressures for more testing for Mad Cow disease. It was a Canadian problem. The US food supply remained safe. Brains and spinal cord fluids didn't contaminate the muscle tissues. Although, the last time she visited a slaughterhouse, she was ten years old, and her father didn't show her everything. Secretary Almond understood the costs, the political costs, her Cabinet position as part of the Administration's team, first and foremost. She also considered the expense and the bad PR for the beef industry and gave these as her reasons. She liked to talk about the safety of the industry whenever a pesky reporter insisted upon bring up Cruetzfeldt-Jakob disease. She rationalized, but if she felt unsure of her own public statements, the long incubation period would give her, and the Administration, any cover they might need. Mad Cow took five to fifteen years to manifest in humans. A different administration would face it.

The first case Dr. Bill Chester saw was an inmate at Susanville. The young doctor worked for a medical group that provided emergency room doctors to places and facilities that have no fulltime doctors. These traveling doctors drive the state for week or two week stints in the isolated areas of California. Dr. Chester ordered tests, but was gone by the time they came back. When he returned the following month, the reports had vanished.

The Susanville docs quickly learned not to ask questions when an inmate was beaten almost to death. If the victim could talk, he reported he "fell out of his bunk." This case was not a beating, so when Dr. Chester learned his patient died, he called the lab where he'd sent the tissue samples. No luck. He called again and reached the technician who ran the test. The technician wouldn't talk to him. Bill Chester confided his concerns to his wife and left for his last assignment at Susanville before leaving the emergency firm. He'd accepted a position with Kaiser Permanente in Santa Clara.

The roads connecting Susanville to civilization ran narrow and long. Even where the road has four lanes, the lonely highway runs down the backside of the Sierras and crosses into Nevada before joining more popular routes. The Highway Patrol said the doctor must have hit an icy patch when he was doing in excess of 90 MPH. They ignored the blue paint on his black Suburban's tailgate and left rear fender.

Bill Chester's widow visited her Senator. Nothing happened for several weeks, until the Senator and a Navy Captain at Walter Reed demanded the lab reports. They broke the silence and reported three cases of suspected Mad Cow in the US, bovine spongiform encephalopathy (BSE). The human variant, Cruetzfeldt-Jakob disease is always fatal.

Next came cases among Navy personnel who had served together aboard a destroyer that traveled between San Diego and the South China Sea five years earlier. The Administration recoiled with outrage about the "premature rush to judgment" and issued elaborate assurances. Secretary Almond ate a steak dinner for the media. The President ate a bowl of beef chili for the cameras at a Colorado rodeo. Bumper stickers blared, Real Americans Eat Beef, but rumors flourished.

Beef sales fell. Canada, with its newly instituted universal testing policy, took over US beef sales to Japan. The US economy hiccuped, then sputtered, as oil prices moved upward and foreign oil workers became targets in Saudi Arabia. Weather-caused disasters hit hard in the Midwest, South and East. When the detainees heard anything of these events, they sounded surreal and remote. Without radio or television, rumors took the place of news, but a few sick jokes surfaced every time a hint of ground beef showed up in the chow.

The women continued to assist with the coffee cultivation. Peach White and the Philippine Red Cross representative moved into a corner of Dugame's Quonset the end of May and took over one of the Dispersing desks. Heavy rains and stormy seas beset the Philippine Archipelago, not yet recovered from Typhoon Nida, the fourth typhoon to hit the islands in the spring of 2004. Thousands of Filipinos remained stranded.

The time drew near, and the goddess could not stop the sky's heavy tears.

Chapter 27

July 2004

The US government extended Across the Board's contract into July. Commander Kenny did not object. Some of the projects the company agreed to construct for the Philippine government were not completed. Even when they used male detainees as laborers, things proceeded slowly. The rains didn't help. Hayhill gave up on the interrogations except for a few last efforts.

"You're not leaving this place until you talk to us, Druid. I'd love to let you go home. You tie my hands." Law Hayhill had his elbows on the table, clasping and unclasping his sweaty hands. He sat across the table from Madison in a bunker-like room with high, useless louvers. The humidity condensed on the walls and formed droplets that trailed down to the floor. The Navy kept supplies in the airless room on the other side of the cement block wall that divided the tiny space.

"Ol' Ev's been very helpful. The two of you could fly away from here together. Maybe as early as day after tomorrow."

"If he's been so helpful, why's he still here?"

Hayhill focused. This one didn't usually respond. "Now, Mrs. Druid, we thought about that. But you see, we have more leverage with you if he stayed. You're holding up the process. It's all on you."

Madison looked at her questioner. Law detected a smirk or a challenge in the woman's face. Her sullen look stated the obvious: You haven't released any talkers. They're still here. She didn't need words.

Hayhill flipped through his papers. "Says here you told your classes, and I quote, 'War is not a value or a tool. War is the failure of reason.' Now that's a little strange coming from a gal who liked to watch *Patton* before important tennis matches."

"I began a week's worth of discussions and lectures in my college freshmen classes with that statement. We fight for our lives, for survival. The problems arise in how we define 'our lives' and how we define 'our survival.' Too bad we can't harness our aggressive tendencies with football, or tennis, and release them that way."

Law Hayhill listened and probed further, but Madison bit her lip and clammed up. She hadn't meant to say anything. Talking to this guy was dangerous. She'd said so more than once in her notes.

Hayhill's conversational tone changed. "I know what you're thinking. Maybe you even hold out hope that the people back home will rise up and demand your release. You and the others. Well, they aren't, you old bitch. There's too few of you. Doesn't matter what the Supreme Court says. Hearings? Ha! No one cares.

Brave soldiers dying in Iraq and Afghanistan. You think anyone cares about a few wild-haired liberals? You think the government has time for Supreme Court hearings? Don't hold your breath." Hayhill stepped back, scratched his neck. A cruel, resolute smile spread across his face. "Well, just thought I might give you a last chance to talk."

Law rubbed his jaw. He noticed Madison's hand on her right knee. "The knee been hurtin'? I could get your prescription, that anti-inflammatory stuff. What's it called?" Madison's expression didn't change. She said nothing.

"We know you were a teacher, a prof. Think you're smart. You know your Constitution, your rights. Well, Madison Druid, I'm here to tell you what you don't know. A big earthquake in California, all kinds of dead, thousands of 'em. There're thousands without power in the Midwest, flooding in the East. The government has no time for seventy-three— Make that seventy of you women. Forgot we lost a few. No time for smart-mouthed old bags on vacation in the warm, sunny Philippines. You get my drift, sweetie? Seventy, plus about a hundred men versus all those thousands of real Americans. Four thousand in Los Angeles alone. You figure it out."

"Four thousand what?" Madison's voice startled Law Hayhill.

"Casualties, you dumb bunny. In Southern California. Four thousand dead or injured, maybe more."

"When?"

"No! No you don't. Tell me what I want to know first." Law sounded irritated. He glanced outside and saw the pesky Red Cross worker heading over. He checked his watch, stood and slammed his chair across the room. Madison raised her fingers in a tiny wave at his back as he stomped down the three steps and out of her life. He had exercised more professionalism and control in the earlier sessions. Something had changed. What Supreme Court decision? Hearings?

* * *

The Filipino workers sympathized with the Americans. Madison noted that they showed it in numerous ways, flowers in a used plastic water bottle, secret smiles, little nods of comfort. This was not Guantanamo or Abu Ghraib prison. After the Navy arrived, there were no other instances of blatant prisoner abuse. Rumors flew. The detainees knew the contingent of contract workers had orders to pull out soon. Madison didn't know where they were headed, and she didn't care. She'd heard that nine detainees, all men, boarded a US transport ship the day before. At least a few Americans would return to the United States. Madison clung to the hope that Ev was among them until Hutch passed the word that Ev was assigned to a work detail at the water purification plant.

Madison picked up the mop bucket, ambled out the door and headed toward the lavatory and shower area, her cleaning assignment for the week. On her way she collected a beetle and a small, beige praying mantis.

No one watched her. Hayhill stomped away toward the flagpole. She took a quick detour into the women's barracks.

The black hen raised her head and clucked when Madison entered. The hen nested between the exterior siding and the interior two-by-fours of the single wall construction where a gap testified to the shortage of materials and the speed with which the compound was built. Two detainees had pounded pieces of scrap lumber into a crude box against the wall. Madison released the insects on the rough concrete floor, and the hen raced after them. She gobbled the beetle, caught the praying mantis on the fly and looked for more. When she saw that was all, she wandered outside to hunt for herself. She had eleven eggs in her clutch. The women decided to let her keep them. Their chow wasn't too bad. Besides, more chickens meant more eggs later. Maybe it was their maternal instincts. Chicken poop was an occasional problem, but the hen rarely ventured into the barracks farther than from her nest to the door.

* * *

Four days after Madison's last interview, the green camouflage-painted Across the Board Corporation helicopter touched down at 1300 hours, and the contractors assembled while it waited. Lt. Dugame, arms folded, observed from the front steps of her office. The few women detainees in the area, eyes fierce, looked up from their chores and watched the men. The women had a sense of anticipation. They waited for the contractors to react. The mother of the girl who was raped was among them, as was a twenty-year old campus activist from Cornell. She gave the contractors their only salute when she adjusted her glasses with her middle finger.

Meese, recovered from his snakebite, brought up the rear. He saw Madison near the lavatory area with her mop and a bucket. He made a little noise, a half-hiss, half-low whistle. Maddy turned and saw his fingers move in a small wave from his hand at his side. She blushed. The corners of her mouth turned up. She opened three fingers of her mop hand in acknowledgement.

One of the other contractors took a last look around, stopped and pointed toward the sky. "Well, damn. Look at that."

Law Hayhill turned to follow the line of sight indicated by the man. Attached to the top of a long, green bamboo pole braced against the women's barracks, flew a white, tee shirt flag with a black hen applique in the center. Law Hayhill spit on the ground.

"Let's get outa here." Law's voice was a bark.

Another of Hayhill's men fantasized aloud about shooting them down with an AK-47. Law leaned out of the helicopter. "I'm going home, and you're still here. Remember that." The helicopter lifted off.

Lieutenant Dugame repressed a laugh, pretended to cough and returned to her office. Unless Singapore was his home, Hayhill wasn't going back to the US. To no one in particular she said, "Better not spit on the sidewalk there, Hayhill, ol' boy."

Over the loudspeaker, the lieutenant announced all hands and detainees assemble for a 1330 briefing at the flagpole. "That's the official flagpole. Work details cancelled for the remainder of the day." She ordered Ensign Regina Loyal and Tia Martinez, the dispersing clerk, to bring the detainee flag to her. She telephoned her counterpart at the men's facility.

"Jim. Maris. I propose a visit of spouses and significant others between our camps. Let's keep the morale headed up. We're here for a long time."

"You can say that again. A discarded, crusty scab flicked into the Pacific. That's what we are. Forgotten. Heard a new rumor, though. This morning. Don't know whether it's credible. Heard Kenny and the rest of us might get orders out."

"What about the detainees? What about Peach, the Red Cross rep?"

"The Red Cross leaves with us. Peach White will get orders out. The detainees, they'd be free to come and go. That's the deal. We get ordered out, and they're stuck."

"Where'd you hear this?"

"Privileged. Can't vouch for it, but with all hell breaking loose stateside, sounds possible.

"The Philippine government will go ballistic. These people have no money. Food leaves with us. We can't abandon these folks!"

"Heard from the same source we'll probably abandon them and call it a screw-up. Say we're real sorry. I e-mailed my congressman today. I know it's against policy. Hell, our careers are over. We talked about this, Maris. You know we've been blown off."

Maris Dugame didn't say anything for several seconds. "I've fourteen women with husbands or others, and one with a cousin, at your camp. Let's set up a meeting in the quad area tomorrow. Let them connect, talk."

"Maris?"

"Yeah?"

"Keep the lid on the rumors, okay?"

"Sure."

* * *

At 1330, the bugler played Reveille, even though it was afternoon. The US flag ran down the flagpole then up again with the black hen tee-shirt flag below it. When the bugler finished, there was silence, then ear-splitting cheering. Cheers, tears and hugs.

Madison worked her way close to Dugame. "Lieutenant, I thank you." Madison placed her hand over her heart, not a formal military salute. She had no hat, and she knew the Navy didn't salute uncovered. Dugame winked.

The noise and celebration died down as the women and a few local guards waited for the briefing. Even the MPs allowed subdued amusement to play across their faces. Everyone had questions, but they held them. Dugame unfolded a packet and started to read. She read the unanimous ruling from the Supreme Court. The detained American citizens were entitled to representation, and a hearing. She said she'd received a dispatch from Captain Kenny at 0700. She told them about the earthquake in California, which they knew, and the killer tornadoes in Illinois and throughout the Midwest, which they did not. Manila was on heightened alert due to a suicide bombing in the city and two on Mindanao. In the US, national emergencies, with unprecedented numbers of casualties, necessitated a delay in the detainees' return to the States. Even though the Supreme Court, in extraordinary emergency session, had issued an opinion favorable to the detainees. The Court determined that as US citizens, the Executive branch had unlawfully denied each detainee's right of habeas corpus, among other rights, but the Court could not bring them home. So, while the grounds for their detention were invalid, they remained detained. No method of releasing them existed. There were a few exceptions.

In addition to the nine men who boarded the transport, sixteen more male detainees boarded a light cruiser on Wednesday, enroute between Taipei and Pearl. Dugame had argued for taking some of the women, but the C.O. said the crowded conditions aboard made any other arrangement unsatisfactory. Kenny didn't back her on this one. The Secretary of Defense apparently felt the men were less a threat than the women, or he was angrier with the women. Madison suspected political influence at work. Several airlines offered their services, but the US government dragged its feet and used the tortured reasoning that while the detainees had won habeas corpus, they could be held pending the availability of judges for hearings.

As the magnitude of the destructive earthquake in Los Angeles became evident, talk of bringing the detainees home ended. All aircraft, ships, emergency and military personnel that the country could spare, found themselves diverted to Los Angeles. Military personnel in Iraq found their time extended, then extended again.

* * *

Peach learned that she had to leave when the US Navy left. She raced into the women's barracks when she heard.

"Madison!" She ran up to her friend and hugged her. "Been ordered out. Navy says I have to leave with them. I have forty-seven dollars." She pulled the bills from her pocket and forced them into Madison's hand. "I worried, Maddy."

"Don't be. At least we're free." Madison indicated the women with her in the barracks.

Peach frowned. "It isn't enough. It's all I had in my purse today."

"Peach, tell our sons we love them. We love them and their families. We hold them in our hearts always."

Peach worried about more than food. In spite of Kenny's orders that detainees receive all necessary shots and medications, supplies had fallen short. She knew how small cuts and insect bites became infected in the tropical climate. There would be no re-supply of medicines. Peach nearly broke down as she looked into Madison's face, but she didn't. Something about Maddy's expression told her Maddy knew, too. Of course, Madison understood all these things.

"Good-bye, dear friend," said Madison. "Thank the tennis group for Ev and me, for all of us here."

A Navy MP appeared in the doorway. "Mrs. White, Your transportation's here."

In spite of her request to stay, the Navy took her with them to Manila and put her on a plane for San Franciso.

* * *

The Filipino people came forward in spite of having little extra. No one asked them. Women showed up at mid-day with baskets and covered containers. They set to work with the former detainees and did the preparation in the kitchen. The Navy had left the equipment in its rapid pullout. When a junior officer questioned leaving so much equipment behind, Kenny replied harshly that stripping the equipment would be a cheap trick not in the spirit of the agreement with the Philippine government. He didn't mention the official protest from the Philippines over leaving the former detainees stranded in their country.

* * *

When asked about the citizen detainees in the Philippines at his news conference on Los Angeles, the President showed some impatience.

"Give us a little time. We'll have hearings. We'll find out what's what. Let's get the domestic disasters under control. We'll get to 'em. Just be calm.

"We have totally innocent women and children, totally innocent people, in this country who need our immediate help. Right now. Think of the folks in Los Angeles. Those in other places in our great country who are suffering. We must deal with the domestic situation first. You all understand that.

"Those folks in the Philippines have shelter. They're not facing tornadoes, floods, fires or an earthquake like LA has. Be calm. That's all I'm askin'."

A questioner in the back of the room shouted something. The President put a hand to his ear. "What's that?"

The President scowled at the questioner. "No, we cannot permit US citizens to travel to Olongapo. We planned to order our personnel out of the area weeks ago, before all this. Listen, we counsel patience. Just as soon as we can, we'll do what's right."

* * *

In Hawaii, on the Big Island, the Earth stayed calm. Mauna Loa's dome continued to expand slightly, and the islands' vents steamed, but the only eruption oozed from the Mother's Day vent opened years earlier. Yet, Kona had the wettest season on record. Every night the Earth cried. The island responded and wore a green gown with black lava seams while it awaited the sea's message.

In June and July the Banana lava flow, named for the banana trees it eliminated, had increased dramatically, but not dangerously. Visitors still hiked to the active flow and watched it pour into the sea. Many Americans ignored politics, and like leaves caught in the lava flow creating new land, civil rights caught fire and died.

Chapter 28

July 2004

Ev wiped his head with a small towel. Madison shook rain from her hair and arms. They'd worn garbage bags with slits for their heads and arms for their walk up the hill to Hutch's home.

"You feel the quake?" Hutch asked. "We had a little shake 'bout fifteen minutes ago."

Ev and Maddy looked up. "No, didn't notice a thing. Of course, we were walking up here, moving ourselves," said Ev. They stood in little pools on Hutch's front porch, pulled off the bags and toweled dry as much as possible. They stowed the garbage bags carefully for their return to the camp. Wonderful aromas of fried rice, Thai noodle soup and limpia drifted through the door and front windows. Clarita had prepared a feast. The smells from the kitchen brightened their day even though Hutch's news was bad.

Hutch told Ev and Madison he couldn't take them to Manila, to the US Embassy as they'd planned. "Too much rain. Have to wait for the mudslides to be cleared.

A couple, three days probably, unless we get more rain. Makes the roads dangerous."

"Don't take any chances, Hutch," said Ev. "You've done so much. Play it safe."

"Yeah. Yeah." Hutch nodded. "No problem."

"You've been so kind," said Madison and hugged him.

Clarita's voice rang out from the kitchen. "Quit hugging my husband. Come and eat."

They all laughed and sat down to the table set with chopsticks and flowers. Madison asked about the delicate white blossoms sprinkled in the center of the dark green tablecloth. "Coffee? I thought coffee bloomed earlier."

"All junk," said Hutch. "All junk this year. So much rain. Flowers and ripe cherry on the same tree. That's why we found all those other projects for you. Never had enough cherry at one time for much coffee." He stared into space, then at the floor and clasped and unclasped his hands. When Clarita brought the platters of food, Hutch inhaled deeply and his expression changed from worry to pleasure.

The two young girls, Leilani and Momi, watched Ev and Madison help themselves to huge portions. The girls' heads swung back and forth from their parents to the Druids.

"Oh, my goodness. Everything smells so good. I took way too much," said Madison. "Been in the camp too long. May I serve you some?" She picked up her plate and scooped a spoonful at a time onto the youngest daughter's plate. "More?"

157

"No thank you, auntie."

Tears welled in Madison's eyes. She looked from the little girl to Hutch in silent acknowledgment of the Hawaiian custom of Ohana, extended family.

Ev held a serving spoon in the air. "Did I take too much?"

Clarita and Hutch insisted he did not, but Madison shot him a quick look. It didn't matter. There was plenty of food. When the meal ended and the light began to slant across the sky, Madison held out her last notes and a packet to their sons. "Thank you for mailing these scribblings, Clarita. We can never reimburse you for all you've done, but we'll try."

Momi, the youngest daughter, showed Maddy and Ev a picture she'd drawn at school in the past year.

"Oh, Momi, tell me about this," said Madison.

"It's from downtown. Magsaysay Drive. Didn't you see it?"

"No, honey. We didn't get to do any sightseeing."

"Turn it over. The teacher wrote on the back."

"Ship's gun from the Oryoku Maru, memorial to the Allied POWs lost when US planes sank the ship December 14, 1944." Maddy read the words aloud and looked to Hutch for more explanation.

"It was a Japanese transport, a hell ship with almost two thousand POW's heading out for Japan. Three hundred men died." Hutch put his arm around his daughter's shoulders.

"It's a good drawing," said Maddy. "We need to remember war is very sad."

"They found the gun in water," said Mori. "I was going to draw the Old Spanish Gate, but the ship's gun was easier. Next time I'll do the gate."

"I see you like to draw. You did a nice job," said Maddy. "Oh, Momi, that reminds me I brought a present for you and Leilani." Madison pulled two tiny white origami cranes from her pocket. "One of the women, Tami Sato, taught us how to fold these cranes. She helped me fold mine. She told me many people believe that if you fold a thousand cranes you'll get one wish. For some, the crane stands for meeting death with defiance, like a samurai."

Madison thought of telling them the story of Sadako Sasaki, a Hiroshima survivor who died of leukemia at the age of twelve, but stopped and instead said, "People say the cranes stand for peace, non-violence and tolerance. For many the crane is a symbol of long life and wishes come true. That is my wish for each of you."

The girls turned the pointy paper cranes over in their hands. Clarita started to speak, but Leilani said, "Thank you, Auntie Maddy." Momi quickly followed her sister's example, and Clarita relaxed.

They finished dinner in time for sunset. The clouds opened and sky caught fire. Even the children stood quietly on the lanai and marveled at the spectacle.

"I never tire of sunsets," said Ev.

"We humans could do worse than worship the sun." Madison spoke softly. "Scatter my ashes in the sea at sunset. That's what I've told my family. Maybe toss in a flower to float along."

"You want, I can drive you back," said Hutch. "Don't want to lose the light."

"No, we'll be fine if Maddy hurries before it starts raining again." Ev looked at the clock in the living area. "Stays light a little longer these days. We can use the time to hold hands and talk," Ev said with an impish grin. He swung Madison's hand to his lips and kissed it.

With another round of hugs, Ev and Maddy stepped into their slippas and departed for the compound. Light was not the problem.

Chapter 29

July 2004

"Oops! Feel that?" Ev slipped, nearly went down.

"Yes. Slippery enough without the ground shaking." Madison slipped with the next jolt. It hit like a quiver, an extended twitch of the Earth. "Ev? This is not good, is it?"

Ev wrapped his forearm around hers and clasped her hand. "Hurry."

Darkness fell. Lights from the compound shown ahead. The noise, a breaking, snapping, flooding roar filled their ears, the Earth's good-bye. The land fell away. Everything on the surface tumbled and collapsed into the mud.

* * *

It was midnight before survivors in the compound jerry-rigged a single floodlight and tried to search for those who might be buried under the rubble. One of the men's barracks had collapsed and slid away. At the women's compound, the shower and toilet area was gone. Their barracks remained but was isolated by huge mudflows on either side. The Philippine government brought in a helicopter the next afternoon, but the one-at-a-time evacuation continued into the next day. Only the main entrance to the women's facility, the men's administration building and the women's administration Quonset escaped damage.

* * *

The landslide spared Hutch and his family. He lost thirty coffee trees on one corner of his property, but he had a feeling that Ev and Madison hadn't made it. Even if they reached the compound, they could have died. At dawn Hutch gathered his family and drove as far as they could toward town. When the road quit, blocked by debris, Hutch, Clarita and the girls picked their way on foot to Clarita's cousin Lupe's home. From there, Hutch and his partner in the machine shop hiked the dangerous terrain around the slide. With canteens on their belts and shovels on their backs, they looked for clues. They searched all day.

"It's hopeless, man," said his partner.

The concentration on Hutch's face gave him a fierce appearance. "Go back, you want. I'm not finished looking."

"Nah, I'm with you. You know. Frustrating is all."

They worked their way down to the compound where part of the mudflow had splintered, eddied and built up along a cement block wall.

Hutch dug where a plastic garbage bag protruded near the edge of the slide. He found a big rubber flip-flop and pulled it from the mud.

"That's one big slippa, man," said his partner.

"I think it's Ev's."

"Maybe. Maybe not. Could have belonged to anyone."

"Looks like da kine he wore to my house."

They dug. After four hours they found two bodies entwined in each other's arms. Hutch stared at the muddy forms, barely human. He wiped away as much gunk as he could, then carefully cleaned the eye wells and the faces with the last of his water. One of Ev's legs was gone. Madison's lower jaw was gone as was her right leg at the knee.

"That knee always gave you lota trouble." Hutch brushed the back of his dirty hand over his right eye. He turned to his partner. "You got the tarp, brah?"

"Yeah. We go with the plan?"

"Yeah. Think so. Boat's not too far. Wait til dark. Take one at a time. Okay?"

"Yeah, brah. Okay."

Hutch cut away a handful of Madison's muddy hair. Ev had no hair. Hutch thought a moment, then wiped his knife on his pants. He started on the wrist, but changed his mind. His partner watched but said nothing. Hutch cut off Ev's left index finger.

"For their family. When the time's right. For their family."

Hutch couldn't bring himself to notify the Philippine authorities. They cremated the dead in pits to stem the outbreak of disease. Estimates of total casualties throughout Luzon ran between two and three hundred, missing, presumed dead. Most of the American detainees had stayed close to the compound and slept there at night, free with nowhere to go. Those who survived the landslide organized a count and tried to ascertain who was missing. Their best guess was thirty-eight to forty-three missing, Ev and Maddy Druid among them.

Chapter 30

Los Altos, March 2006

A flock of ravens awoke late and took to the air with their noisy chatter. Fog dimmed the early light until the sun rose and evaporated the sea-scented moisture. One of the thick-billed birds remained on its roost, neck outstretched in the damp air. It seemed to be listening.

* * *

The memorial over, Peach lingered. She helped more than was necessary. Cynthia, Sue and Peach remained. When it became obvious she would not get Cynthia alone, Peach took a deep breath. "Cyn, I didn't realize how tactless I was back when this all started."

"Peach, what in the world are you talking about? You've done more than all of us put together."

"I mean the tennis remarks. About my being better than you. It really hit me when you read that part."

"Peach…"

"Tennis was so important to me. It saved my sanity in the beginning of all the stuff with Jack. I was in shock when he left."

"Peach, don't…"

"I know I've always been blunt. I'm sorry. That's all. I wanted to tell you I'm sorry."

"We love you for your honesty, Peach. Even when it hurts sometimes."

Peach glanced at Sue who nodded assent and smiled.

"Thanks," said Peach. She glanced at her watch. "Did I mention a friend of mine from the Philippines will be here next week? I need to go. I have a tango lesson in fifteen minutes."

* * *

Cynthia took out the garbage with the disposable vacuum cleaner bag that contained crumbs and pulverized ashes from the fireplace. She looked around the clubhouse one last time. Everything was back in place. The flowers, linens, silver, china, the food, all packed up and gone and manuscripts secreted away, unmentioned. Sue returned from taking a box to her car. She and Cynthia stopped a moment.

"I thought this…" Cynthia extended her arm. "I thought today would be a final good-bye, but I feel haunted." She locked the clubhouse door.

When Cynthia turned toward her, Sue looked away and said, "Maybe there are no final good-byes."

In the parking lot Cynthia spoke softly. "Maddy knew who betrayed her, didn't she?"

"Very possibly. I think she did, but it doesn't matter. She expressed no enmity, none. You heard Peach. She doesn't gloss over things. Peach would probably say, if she thought about it."

The women hugged and said they'd see each other at tennis Thursday. A utility van drove into the parking lot as Sue headed out. She watched from her rearview window and saw Cynthia speak briefly with the driver.

"Explains a lot, Cyn. You knew they were listening." Sue whispered to herself. Her car hesitated at the top of the drive. Cynthia turned toward her and raised a hand in a small wave, hidden from the van by her body.

* * *

Cynthia drove the short distance home. A light on the dashboard indicated her trunk was not latched. She didn't notice. The garage door stood open, but Cynthia pressed the garage door opener when she pulled into her driveway. Down came the garage door and frightened her. She paid attention this time and pressed the switch again. She opened the trunk, then decided not to unload right away. The purple foil gift bag from Peach lay on top. Cynthia knew what was inside without opening hers. Each of them received three ounces of vacuumed packed Philippine coffee beans, medium roast, from Hutch's farm. She untied the ribbon and sniffed the rich aroma that came through in spite of the packaging. Noises in the backyard distracted her.

She followed the sounds to a bird, a huge raven squatting on the ground near the composter. Cynthia moved cautiously to within ten feet. The bird in its glistening black-plumage clearly expected her to feed it and chat. The raven used pleasant tones, no beak clattering, no shrill protests, no caws or ruffled feathers of disgust. The raven shrugged its shoulders and addressed Cynthia directly. It blinked at her. It turned its head to one side and back several times and kept up its series of chirps and calls and shoulder shrugging.

Cynthia talked back. When Jason came out and found Cynthia in the backyard, she called softly to him and said, "Come see this. It's talking to me."

The bird continued, unperturbed.

Jason approached. "Nevermore?"

"Maybe its evermore," said Cynthia. "Friends evermore." She tilted her head, so did the bird. "Madison forgave me."

Cynthia tore a corner off the packet in her hand and tossed one of the precious coffee beans to the raven. The bird studied the bean a moment, then ate it and talked and shrugged its shoulders some more. A gunshot-like sound from a road crew a block away frightened the raven. Another sharp crack followed. The raven took a half step, a hop, unfolded its four-and-a-half-foot wingspan and glided over the fence. Part of one tail feather was gone. Old bird, like me, Cynthia thought.

Jason unloaded the car. He didn't see her drop the manuscript in the composter and dump the morning's coffee grounds on top. In the afternoon, Sue called and asked Cynthia if she had time for a walk.

"A walk?"

"Yes. Doesn't have to be long. I thought it would be fun. A fresh start."

They strolled to Loyola Corners, a half-mile away, and stopped for a cold drink. They each grabbed a straw and carried their tall, lidded plastic cups of iced tea outside. They sat in the shade. A teenager in a vintage red Mustang convertible nodded to his music in the parking lot. It wasn't too loud. Cynthia and Sue seemed lost in their own thoughts. Sue heard something called *Yoshimi Battles the Pink Robots* and glanced askance at the young man.

Cynthia saw Sue's look and said, "Kind of a vague '60's feeling, yet not."

Sue gave Cynthia the same look, then smiled. "You mean protest music?" Cynthia didn't answer.

While the women sat, Mike Doughty sang *Move On*. Laurel Cantrell sang *Sam Stone,* and Tom Waits sang *Day After Tomorrow*. The women traded a bit of small talk. When they finished, Foothill Expressway, in the background, provided white noise for their walk home. Sue gave Cynthia all the time she needed. And at last, Cynthia brought up the topic she'd avoided yet wanted to discuss.

"How did you know? You knew, didn't you, before I said anything? Did the others know?"

"You pretty much gave it away today, Cyn. I think Kate knows. She's sharp, doesn't miss a thing. Me? I picked up on lots of little clues you dropped all along.

Sometimes I heard a vibration, something odd. I would or wouldn't hear your authoritative Texas drawl. It comes out when you're deadly serious. Took me awhile to catch the changes. The circumstances were so bizarre. And, suspicion and knowledge are different."

She saw worry lines on Cynthia's face. "Leave it alone, Cyn. What you did today atones for a lot. You worked hard on Maddy's notes and all those interviews. You wove a story for us, an important story."

She could see Cynthia didn't feel any better, so she tried again. "Besides, Peach would say something like, 'When the reward for courageous leadership is banishment and death, not too many people step up.' We all must search our souls."

"The man …" Cynthia's voice sounded far away. "The man whose wallet I found, and then a second man and a woman, three of them. They threatened my children." Her voice rose, pleading. "They said they'd never find jobs. That they would put them on a do not employ list." Cynthia looked to Sue for understanding. Sue waited.

Cynthia rolled her lips into her mouth and twisted her fingers. "They asked lots of questions. Nothing made sense. It was like they had a deadline." Cynthia stopped, expelled a whoosh of air. She shook her head and closed her eyes. "I guess they did. Their questions hit me like machine gun bullets. There was something about protests. Did I know anyone who ever protested."

They stood by Sue's car in front of Cynthia's house. Sue touched her arm. "It's over."

"No, it's not."

Cynthia promised to call Sue if she needed to talk, and she watched Sue's car disappear. A raven called from a tall deodora. Cynthia sniffed, wiped the back of her hand across her nose and stood straighter. She went into her backyard and took a deep breath. "No, it's not over."

She picked a Morning Glory blossom and tucked it behind her ear then she rescued Madison's story. She wiped off the coffee grounds and mailed the stained pages to Madison's eleven-year-old granddaughter.

About the Author

Linda Lanterman understands political power. She held both appointed and elected office in California. Her rich sense of character developed early. As a Navy Junior, she finished high school in Sasebo, Japan. She attended schools in nine states and crisscrossed the rest. Her parents taught her to notice everything, to see how power and prejudice mingle and to examine her own presumptions. She holds her Bachelor's degree from the University of California, Berkeley and her Master's from the University of Georgia, Athens, where she taught freshman political science.

As a teacher she became a master storyteller who made history and government come alive with her eye for motive, unintended consequences and her belief in knowledge as the best foundation for power.

Lanterman has written five novels, *The Writing Lesson*, *Not Nice*, *Release Me*, *Transition in Green* and *Stain*. She is one of the Sierra Writers. She divides her time between California's Sierra foothills and Kailua-Kona, Hawaii.

Printed in the United States
25733LVS00002B/1-78